ABEL SMITH OF NANTUCKET

H. BEDFORD-JONES

ABEL SMITH
OF NANTUCKET

H. BEDFORD-JONES

COVER BY
RUDOLPH BELARSKI

ILLUSTRATIONS BY
FRED HUMISTON

ALTUS PRESS • 2014

TABLE OF CONTENTS

I

ABEL SMITH OF NANTUCKET

With Nearly Thirty Whalers and Merchant
Ships Anchored in the Bay, Crews Had
Money to Spend in Yerba Buena

S MITH WALKED awkwardly into the small, untidy morning-crowded store of Captain Leidesdorff. He was shock-headed and his clothes were too small for him—he had landed only an hour ago—but one forgot this at second glance. He had a bony face, older than his twenty-two years, with two bright blue eyes whose sparkle was alert and friendly and impudent, catching the attention very pleasantly.

The store was busy; it was always busy these days. The permanent population of the town was fast swelling—it was over a hundred now. With nearly thirty whalers and merchant vessels anchored in the bay, crews had money to spend. Marines from the garrison and sailors from the *Portsmouth* had money to spend. Rancheros and hunters and settlers from across the bay had money to spend, or the equivalent.

No need of inquiring for the proprietor here; he was self-announcing. Smith passed to the railed-in office at the back of the store, whence resounded a stentorian bellow, and gazed at the brawny, swarthy figure. A seafaring mulatto from the Danish West Indies, Leidesdorff had been vice-consul here until the United States flag was raised, two months ago.

HIS OFFICIAL services were thus ended, but he was still the most important person in Yerba Buena, next to Lieutenant Bartlett of the *Portsmouth*, who was acting as alcalde or mayor until the town got re-organized. The war with Mexico was still in effect in this September of '46, but the fighting was all in the

south around Los Angeles, and Yerba Buena was far too busy with its own affairs to pay the least attention to it.

Leidesdorff turned suddenly, met the gaze of Smith, and erupted.

"Well, who are you? Who are you staring at?"

"You," said Smith composedly. "You're Captain Leidesdorff, aren't you? My name's Abel Smith of Nantucket; worked my passage here on the whaler *Nancy T.* that anchored yesterday. I'm going to stay in California for good, and I was told you might be able to give me a job."

"Oh! And what kind of a job are you looking for, Mr. Smith?" came the lusty roar.

"Any kind. Here in your store or anywhere. I'm right handy with tools or figures, either one."

Leidesdorff, whose heart was as big as his voice but under better control, chewed at his Manila cigar and eyed the applicant shrewdly.

"So you mean to stay here. Hm! Worked your passage; good. Speak your piece and no beating around the bush; better still. Young fellow, too. Everybody's young here; O'Farrell is only twenty-four. All but me. I'm an old fellow, going on thirty-five. This is a young man's town. Got any money to invest?"

"No, sir. Only two dollars," Smith replied, his blue eyes dancing pleasantly.

"Can't afford to buy yourself decent clothes, eh? Not that they matter here."

"I'll need to eat worse than I need new clothes," said Smith.

Leidesdorff rumbled out a laugh. This appealed to him. Eating was one purpose of his existence.

"I'm building the biggest house in town. Heaven knows when it'll be done. And I'm building a wharf, the first one in Yerba Buena. I can employ you, yes. But you used your hands to get here. Have you got a head to use? Let's see. You're a Yankee, eh? Come in and sit down. We'll soon find out."

Smith obeyed the gesture, entered the enclosure, and took the chair indicated. He accepted the fat black cigar shoved at him and sat in some astonishment as Leidesdorff spoke in a confidential bellow which dropped, at crucial instants, almost to a whisper.

"The brig *Constantine* of Boston reached Monterey yesterday and comes on here; she might get here today, certainly tomorrow, depending on the wind, understand?"

"No, sir," replied Smith. "Not yet."

"All right. Go find Frank Ward. He's a competitor of mine— got here in July and is doing a good business already, Smart

New Yorker; young fellow like you. The cargo, dammit, is consigned to him; he arranged for it before he left New York in February. I need it badly. He won't sell to me at any price; he knows I need it. And I've got ten thousand dry hides, not to mention tallow, piling up in my warehouse; can't get shipment out. Cruel, that's what it is, cruel!"

Leidesdorff paused to swear hotly in mingled English, French and Danish. As a former sea-captain, he was highly competent at this. He puffed his cigar alight and added a few choice Spanish expletives for good measure.

"I suppose Mr. Ward knows the ship is coming?" Smith asked innocently.

"No, dammit! Larkin at Monterey works with me; he sent me word."

"Oh!"

"Well, what are you waiting for?"

"You haven't said what you want me to do."

"Buy that cargo for me, or any part of it!" roared the captain. "Lie him out of it, cheat him out of it, rob him, do anything you blasted please—prove whether or not you have any brains. Price is no object. Get part of that cargo!"

Smith glanced down at himself. "In these clothes? I've outgrown them and—"

"Hm!" Leidesdorff scribbled on a bit of paper and handed it over. "Give that to my clerk. Outfit yourself on credit. Everything's credit here."

"Thank you, sir." Smith rose, shook hands, and departed.

AT THE front of the store he did business with a clerk, thoughtfully trading in his old garments, which were sound and had value here. He obtained a new outfit, and carefully transferred the fat Manila cigar to his jacket pocket, with a few other personal possessions. He was, of necessity, traveling light. As he left the store he was thinking over the merchant's words—well over them and around them, in fact; a habit he had. Often, words went over his head and left him with brand new ideas to think about.

Smith, in his little time ashore, had picked up all sorts of information. Now he made for John Henry Brown's saloon, which was a sort of gossip exchange and realty board for Yerba Buena. The alcalde, Bartlett, was there, being engaged in selling one of the most expensive town lots, a twenty-five-dollar one, to a newcomer from across the plains. It had to be done here because the only town plat was kept behind Brown's bar for general reference. Bartlett was quite angry about this and was arguing with Brown about it.

THE ALCALDE departed and Smith talked with John Henry Brown, who loved to talk, and asked him about Frank Ward. John Henry was English. He relished gossip, and threw out mysterious hints about his own noble birth and titled ancestors, but he was a very pleasant man, and he knew everything about everybody in Yerba Buena.

Frank Ward was a fine young chap, said he, who had come west with money in his pocket and bade fair to be a success. He lacked the advantages of Leidesdorff or of Grimes & Davis, or even of Mellus & Howard, said advantages then being discussed in some detail, with a bit of attention to prices and so forth.

Getting enough of this. Smith finally set forth to find Frank Ward's new shop, soon to supplant his first place of business. This was being knocked into shape in an old adobe structure near the beach of the cove on which Yerba Buena stood.

Smith found his man bossing the workers, mostly Americans newly arrived. There were few Californians in the place, but immigrants were pouring into the country rapidly and of these many found their way to the town on the great bay. Ward was a young man, vigorous and able, with a cheerful smile and a winning frankness that had already made him popular.

"My name's Abel Smith, Mr. Ward. Can you give me a few minutes?"

"Surely can," said Ward. "Come on outside. Can't talk with these carpenters at work. I'm glad of a breath of air."

THEY LEFT the building, walking a little down the sandy street. Before them was the cove, beyond that the western stretch of the bay. The lofty heights of Sausalito and Table Hill, across the Golden Gate, lifted far along the sky. Spars of ships dotted the waters, boats were toiling back and forth, and off to the right the Contra Costa hills blotted the horizon.

Ward filled a pipe. Smith repressed a kindred inclination, and instead produced the fat Manila cigar and mouthed it, as being more impressive. In that bony face, it was.

"You a stranger in town?" asked Ward.

Smith nodded. "Just arrived and looking for business, but I've been using my eyes a bit. Looks to me like you were up against a bad combination here, Mr. Ward."

"I? Well, I wasn't aware of it. In just what way?"

"Opening a store. On the one hand you have Grimes & Davis, with Grimes a settled Honolulu merchant, able to throw all sorts of business to this branch concern here. On the other you have Leidesdorff, who works with Larkin at Monterey— Larkin, former American consul and the biggest business man in the country. A millionaire, they say."

"Can't hurt me," said Ward. But, as he lighted his pipe, he eyed the young stranger critically. A pleasant fellow, certainly, and filled with energy; keen Yankee trader type.

"Well, let's see. You need goods for your store, don't you?"

"I could use them."

"All right. Suppose a ship stops at Honolulu, as most ships do en route here, or at Monterey the capital. In either case, you've no partner there to shunt her cargo on to you. Therefore, you're working at a disadvantage."

"But I have agents in the east who can consign me cargoes direct," said Ward. "Not but what your argument is sound, Smith."

"I see," said Smith.

"I've done enough business in my temporary quarters to know what I'm doing," went on Ward amiably. "And when my new place gets in shape, you'll see that I'll get my full share of business."

"If you have the merchandise to offer, yes. That's the rub out here—getting the stuff," Smith rejoined sagely. "Also, return shipments. Now, let's suppose that you had a ship on the way here. What would you send back in her?"

"I wouldn't have to send anything. If I could give her a freight, so much the better. Of course, the main exports are hides and tallow."

Abel Smith chewed at his cigar.

"Would you be interested in picking up a likely lot?" he asked. "Somewhere between five and fifteen thousand hides, and tallow in accordance, at five per cent under the usual going price here?"

Ward gave him a sharp look. "Might be. Let's go over to Brown's and have a drink."

"Don't drink, thanks," said Smith. "Not unless necessary. I don't mind saying that I like your looks, Ward. I know of something that *might* improve the looks of your new store, too."

"What's that?" asked Ward, with an amused air.

"Wait, now. Not so fast. You spoke of consignments from the East. Have you got any such consignments coming, or was that just big talk?"

"I have a cargo on the way—somewhere this side of Cape Horn, I hope. Why?"

"Just wanted to know. Some folks do a lot of brag without any base for it. But I'd take your word. Now, look at that storefront of yours. Going to put your name on it?"

"I hope so, as soon as I get a man to paint the sign."

"Well, the name of Frank Ward would look all right. But people will do more trading with two names than with one. They figure two fellows in business together have tried out each other's honesty and so forth; it's human nature to put reliance where reliance already exists."

"Maybe you're right." Ward smiled. "Just what are you driving at?"

THE BRIGHT blue eyes went to him, twinkling. "Ward & Smith might look pretty good on that new sign. Save the expense of painting on an extra name later, too."

"Oh! Are you proposing a partnership?" Ward exclaimed.

"Well, in a way," rejoined Smith thoughtfully. "Having a partner would save hiring a clerk. Also, you should have an outside man to drum up goods for export and make connections and so forth. Say, a quarter interest, until I'm able to buy another quarter and make it a full partnership."

Ward puffed at his pipe for a moment. "Hm! I don't know you—"

"I don't know you any better," cut in Smith, "but I'm satisfied already."

"Thanks." Ward chuckled softly. "Just what are you prepared to offer? Actual cash is almost unknown out here."

"Two things. First, you say that you have a cargo on the way out. I'll guarantee to take half that cargo off your hands on arrival, at your usual profit expectation. How much over cost might that be?"

Ward, like most of the active spirits in town, was in his early twenties. He was by no means averse to quick decisions and snap judgments. His notion of profits, particularly in large deals, was naturally unadjusted as yet to the standards of the country; he was only two months in residence.

"Well, I reckon ten per cent would be a fair profit," he replied.

"All right. You agree to sell me half the cargo at that profit. I'll agree to get you the tallow and hides I mentioned, for export shipment, at five per cent off market price. A dry hide here brings a dollar fifty, and in Boston four to five dollars; you'll have a nice fat profit right there."

Ward nodded, mentally totting up the fatness with much pleasure.

"Further," went on Abel Smith, chewing the unlit cigar judiciously, "I've been figuring winds and sailing speeds very carefully. Within the next two days, might even be tonight or tomorrow, I'm expecting a ship to arrive in whose cargo I'll have a quarter-interest. It's mostly trade knicknacks such as are in demand out here. I'll hand over that interest to you gratis, plus the profit you'll make on the hides and tallow, to pay for my one-fourth share in your business."

WARD BIT on his pipestem for a reflective moment, while Smith inspected the ships out in the bay, and the small boats plying back and forth, and the *Portsmouth* lying across at her anchorage in the Sausalito bight. It was clear to him, very happily clear, that Frank Ward had not the slightest idea he was talking about the brig *Constantine*. There was no reason for Ward to suspect it, of course; there must be none.

"Hm! Well, I don't see anything wrong with your offer," replied Ward at length. "But now look here, Smith. No man alive can figure on the arrival of a ship on this coast within weeks or months, let alone days. Not when a ship must come around Cape Horn and lie at the mercy of winds and tides for long periods. It can't be done. I have a ship on the way here myself, and haven't the least idea when she'll arrive. So how can you claim to know?"

Smith met the questing gaze, removed the dear from his mouth, and winked one blue eye solemnly.

"I'm a smart Yankee, Mr. Ward. Maybe I just guess. Maybe I have advance information on winds and tides. I'm making you this proposal for immediate decision today—say, three o'clock this afternoon. If you don't like the notion, others might, and I want to know. So I'll come around and get your answer then, eh?

"And I'm prepared," he added, "in case the ship I mention does not arrive within two days, to call off the whole deal; this may be written into the agreement. Think it over and you may conclude that if I do have inside information, or if I am such a good guesser, as you may prefer—then I'll be a valuable adjunct to the firm. Glad to have met you, sir. See you this afternoon."

With a firm, brisk handshake, Abel Smith departed.

HE DID not go back to Leidesdorff's place; he could very easily guess that with Yerba Buena small as it was, every stranger was noted and his movements known, curiosity being a natural quality here as elsewhere. So he nosed about the town, spent some time lingering in the comparatively small establishment of Mellus & Howard, and shortly after noon sauntered toward the new house Leidesdorff was occupying while it was building.

It was a house of some size, by far the largest in town, and by local standards very handsome. Captain Leidesdorff was at noon meat, enjoying himself to the utmost; with him was a guest, a gay Irishman named O'Farrell, who had tried ranching up Sonoma way and was almost decided to pitch it over and cast in his fortune with Yerba Buena.

The table groaned under salt salmon, beef in various kinds, venison, elk steaks sent down from Sutter's fort, vegetables in variety, Spanish dishes, Russian dishes, and wines in profusion. The worthy captain had a good cook. He also had an Indian boy and girl to look after the table and his house, with others on the way. Sutter supplied his friends with redskin urchins, trained and housebroke and even speaking some English; and Sutter was a bosom pal of the captain.

Smith was brought in—as he had hoped—introduced to O'Farrell, and planted at the table. Honest Leidesdorff had certain habits of which Larkin, in consular days, had tried vainly to break him.

"Fill up, my friend!" he bellowed lustily. "Here is some splendid Bordeaux—claret, the English call it—of an admirable vintage; it cost me three dollars the bottle. And you must taste this salt salmon. Sutter sends it down from the Sacramento. He salts it up there, and do you know what the rascal charges for it? Twenty dollars the barrel—yes, sir, twenty! I sell it to the Russian ships for thirty, so that is all right. Pitch in!"

He turned to O'Farrell and jerked a thumb at Smith.

"Arrived today, off that whaler that came in—and is going to stay! I set him a job to do and promised to employ him if he fulfilled it." Leidesdorff rumbled with hearty laughter. "A job, yes! To buy for me half the cargo that Frank Ward is expecting from the east. Ho, ho!"

He went off into a peal of laughter.

Smith, who was attacking everything in sight, looked up. "You said to buy it, price no object."

"So I did, so I did!" roared Leidesdorff. "Can you imagine it, Jasper? This boy, just arrived in town today, this bright lad, buying half the cargo from Ward for me—for old Leidesdorff! Ward would cut off his right arm first."

"Did it," said Smith, his mouth full.

"Eh?" The captain, wine-glass in hand, paused. "What's that you said?"

"Bought it for you."

Leidesdorff stared. His mouth opened, he sat as though transfixed, his eyes bulging at Smith, who went on eating, being ravenous. O'Farrell looked at the captain and fell to laughing; he went into a gale of mirth until he had to wipe the tears from his eyes.

"Oh, it'll be the death of me!" he gasped. "The bright lad, says you—and be damned if it ain't the truth! Buy it, says you, price no object—and out he goes and does it! Probably signed up as your agent to pay Ward a hundred or a thousand per cent profit—price no object, says you! And I just now heard you confirm it, so you can't back out—ho, ho! And you the smartest man in Yerba Buena—stuck for it!"

At this, Leidesdorff began to be agitated. He gulped his wine. He turned purple in the face. He roared enormous oaths in

Danish and German. Then, being really concerned, he ceased to bellow and spoke in a low voice.

"Smith, lad! You didn't play me such a trick, you with the honest face of an angel! You wouldn't do that to old Leidesdorff. Did you really buy it?"

Smith, busy eating, nodded and helped himself to more of the fried beef.

"For the love of heaven, what did you pay? Do you know that I'm bound by what you did?" cried Leidesdorff. "You wouldn't ruin me, lad? How much did you pay? What will it cost me?"

"Twenty per cent over his cost," said Smith.

"What? Twenty per cent?" Leidesdorff s fist came down on the table and the dishes jumped and clattered. The swarthy features beamed. "No more! Splendid! That is wonderful! Muchacho! A bottle of champagne. Three bottles!"

"Thanks, none for me," said Smith. "I don't drink, Captain."

It was a merry meal all around; Smith was full fed for the first time in months. He had not relished whale meat. He did no more talking until a fresh box of Manila cigars was opened— two dollars the box, said Leidesdorff—and he lighted one. He refused the offered brandy, took a folded paper from his pocket, and handed it to his host.

"What's this?" the captain demanded.

"For you to sign, please. And fill in the amount of tallow and hides."

Leidesdorff opened the paper. His eyes dilated. He burst into full voice.

"What?" His bellow could have been heard at Sausalino. "My hides? My tallow? Sell to you at ten per cent less than the current market? Are you crazy?"

O'Farreli began to chuckle once more.

"It's part of the bargain," Smith explained innocently. "You were glad that I got the half cargo so cheap; you said so. This will make it cost just a little more. Of course, if you don't want to do it, that's all right."

"Sell my hides less than the market price? Of course I don't want to," stormed the captain. "Am I a fool, young man?"

Smith's blue eyes twinkled. "No, no. It's all right," he said. "Mellus & Howard are not such important merchants as you are, but they'll be glad to take over that half-cargo of knick-nacks, and pay even more."

"Wait, young man, wait. You have a devil inside you, I think! You pinch old Leidesdorff who is kind to you—"

"Oh, no!" said Smith in protest. "I could charge you much more; I'm not doing that, and you don't have to pay me any commission either. The hides take care of that."

LEIDESDORFF BLINKED at him. Jasper O'Farrell once more went off into an explosion of laughter.

"Bright boy, says you! Now it's a young man he is—oh, captain dear, you'll be the death of me yet! I'd like to be on hand when you grant the young fella the status of a man full grown—"

"Shut up!" growled Leidesdorff. "Muchacho! Bring the pens and ink."

He signed the paper and thrust it at Smith, who smiled and pocketed it. Then he shook his finger at the young man warningly.

"You stay away from Mellus & Howard, do you understand that? They are fine fellows, and we are friends; just the same, Larkin has put money into that firm, and I know it. Larkin is a smart man. He plays everybody's game."

"Did he send them word too, about the *Constantine?*" plumped out Smith.

"No. He plays only one man's game at a time, otherwise he would not be smart. But you keep away from those fellows or you'll get your nose bit off, savvy?"

The meal was protracted, but Smith did not mind. Leidesdorff talked with huge gusto, as he did everything. There was meat to his words; they were well worth hearing. He could paint more of the conditions of the country in five minutes than one could learn elsewhere in days. He had a finger in everything and knew everyone intimately, and knew the reasons for everything.

Smith tore himself away barely in time to keep his three o'clock appointment.

Oddly, it was a relief to find himself back with the New Yorker. Frank Ward was his own kind; he had liked Ward on first sight, and knew himself liked in return. Ward took him by the arm and led him out of the hammering to a small room where they could be alone.

"I've been thinking over your proposals, Smith," said Ward in his brisk, cheerful fashion. "About those hides and tallow—how much can you supply? When deliver?"

"Ten thousand hides, seventy hogsheads of tallow. Delivered tomorrow if you like."

Ward whistled thoughtfully. "You must have been scouring the ranch country! Nobody here would have such quantities, except Leidesdorff, who stands in with the Vallejo crowd. Unless you're getting them from Sutter."

"I told you," Smith said quietly, "that it'd pay you to have a partner who could drum up business. This is a cattle country and nothing else; everybody agrees it's good for nothing else. I'm not so sure. A lot of American farmers are flocking in; some day it may do better. But right now, hides and tallow are the exports, and they're not to be found by sitting in Yerba Buena and expecting them to grow here."

Ward nodded complete comprehension.

"Right. Well, my friend, it's a deal. When shall we write out the articles?"

"Now," Smith said in his laconic way.

"Need a lawyer?"

"I can protect myself. Can't you? Go ahead; you write 'em out."

Smith smiled and picked up a pen. "All right. As of this date, you have a quarter interest in the firm of Ward & Smith. Conditional upon your delivery to me within one week of this tallow and hide consignment at five per cent under the local market. Also, conditional upon your delivery within two days, to our joint account, of a quarter interest in the cargo of a ship named—what name?"

"Next ship to arrive here. Make it read that way," said Smith.

Ward gave him a smile and paused. "I'll not hold you to this two-day condition if you want to get out of it."

"Stick it in. You may be glad you did."

Ward shrugged and scraped away nimbly. Then he paused again, glancing up.

"Conditional further," he added, "on your taking up one-half the cargo of the brig *Constantine,* consigned to me, upon her arrival here; you to pay ten per centum over cost. Correct?"

"Correct," said Smith. "I'd like you to make me a separate memorandum regarding that half-cargo. You don't know what the sum will come to, I suppose?"

"Can't tell till she arrives and we get the invoices."

Ward continued with his scribbling. When all was done, Smith read over the writing, nodded agreement, picked up the pen and signed. Then he held out his hand.

"Shake!" he said. "That's the sort of a bargain I set more store by. Anybody can break a contract if he's got a mind to squirm around the written word. If a handshake ain't binding, nothing is."

Ward shook hands heartily, and winced.

"My lord, but you've got a horny grip! You know, Smith, I like your style. I think we'll get on. Won't you come over to John Henry's and wet our bargain?"

Smith shook his head. "Later; not now. I want nobody to know about this for a few days—until you get the sign painted and ready to hang."

"All right," said Ward. "Where are you staying in town?"

Smith hesitated. "I've been too busy to think about that. I don't know yet—only came off the ship this morning. That Nantucket whaler."

"Well, suppose you come around about six. We'll have supper together, and I can put you up on a pallet in the back room, until you get located; eh?"

"Thanks," said Smith. "I'll be here. Know anybody at Monterey?"

"No. Why?"

"We ought to have someone there to act for us and send word by fast messenger of all ship arrivals there—then we'd be forewarned. Might be well worth while."

"By Jove, yes! That's an idea." Ward broke off, comprehension twinkling in his eyes. "Hello! Is that how you knew about your ship being due to arrive?"

"Maybe," said Smith, smiling.

The other clapped him on the back. "Good man! We'll get on. Look here—suppose she doesn't arrive, and our agreement falls through?"

"Then," said Smith, "you set a price on the quarter interest and I'll pay it."

"Agreed. You'll trust me to set a fair price, will you?"

"Yes."

Upon this, they parted.

AFTER ANOTHER circuitous course, Smith came into the Leidesdorff emporium and settled down in the office with the captain. He very frankly appealed to the older man for advice, laying his cards on the table—that is, most of them. One card he held out. He said nothing about his partnership agreement with Frank Ward, having the quite correct conviction that the subject would be unpleasant, and at the present stage of affairs, unprofitable. The lusty captain, whose quarrels with all and sundry were notorious, never indulged in halfway measures. He had quarrelled violently with Bob Ridley, port captain under the .late Mexican regime; and Ridley, in consequence, had been the only local casualty of the change of government, and now cooled his heels behind the bars of Sutter's fort.

Upon all other points, Abel Smith was entirely frank, even detailing his prospective profits. Leidesdorff expanded, took a fresh cigar, and regarded him with jovial admiration.

"Young man, you remind me of myself when I was your age! Now, let's see. You contract to buy my hides and tallow at ninety per cent; you sell them at ninety-five. I'll deliver on credit until you collect from your buyer, Ward. Hm! You buy Ward's half-cargo at ten percent over his cost, selling to me at twenty—pay with a draft on me. Merciful God! Do you realize how much money that will amount to?"

"No. I've not the slightest idea of his cargo's value."

"It'll be thousands—thousands!" said the captain impressively.

"I hope so. Now advise me about the details—the draft on you and so forth."

"Wait! I must go tomorrow in the launch to Sutter's fort; I must see Sutter about many business details. Let this wait until I get back—"

"No. That would be a week or ten days," objected Smith, "This affair must be closed at once, before the *Constantine* arrives. Otherwise it might fall through and you'd lose that merchandise. We can write out any papers here and now."

"All right, all right," rumbled Leidesdorff. "You know, there's no bank here, very little actual money; everything is done by credits and paper and drafts and so forth. Everybody is in debt. I am in debt. How much? I don't know. Maybe twenty, thirty thousand. Sutter is deeper, maybe a hundred thousand. It does not matter. So we'll close the deals now."

As the pen scratched, Abel Smith felt very happy about it all. He had landed this morning with two dollars in his pocket; now he would be in funds—maybe. The papers were written out and signed; so far as Leidesdorff was concerned, all was well. This took time, of course.

"Look, young man!" said the captain. "You are smart. I knew it from the first. You shall work for me; I can use you, as I promised—"

"As soon as you return from Sutter's fort, we'll talk it over," put in Smith hastily. "You've done much for me, and I'm grateful. Let it rest until you're back. Where's that order for your hides and tallow—oh, here it is. All's correct."

"All right, but you shall have a good job with me," began the captain. Just then along came O'Farrell, full of business affairs which Smith found vastly interesting.

THE IRISHMAN, young as he was, had knocked about in Mexico and South America, and had picked up a knowledge of surveying. Leidesdorff was trying to promote an agitation for a totally new survey of Yerba Buena, to be made by O'Farrell, the old one having been a primitive Mexican affair. This was, however, a matter to be handled with diplomacy, and also with an eye to variously owned lots and properties. Abel Smith listened carefully to all that was said. The survey would be well in the future, but ideas sprang quickly to mind and might be useful later.

Leidesdorff, for example, had a wild but profound conviction that the town might in time run as far as the old mission, two and a half miles south, and as far west over the sandhills toward the Pacific shores. This was lunacy but O'Farrell encouraged it. As they talked, a man came in, panting and breathless.

"News, Leidesdorff!" he cried. "There's a ship coming in through the Gate, a brig! She'll be in and anchored before turn o' the tide!"

Smith hurriedly took his chance to get away, for it was close to six. If this news spread, if the brig were identified by her signals, he would have breakers ahead.

He found Frank Ward in the silent store; the workmen had departed. And Ward had heard the news; he was wildly excited.

"Have you heard? Have you heard, Smith? A brig's coming in between the heads now! She's the *Constantine*, my brig! She'll be in port tonight!" He laughed eagerly. "Afraid that kills our agreement, doesn't it?"

"Why?" asked Smith.

"Well, you claimed your ship would strive within two days—"

"Next ship to arrive," Smith corrected him. "It's worded that way. My part of the agreement will be fulfilled. You're to have my quarter share of her cargo, gratis."

Ward regarded him with a puzzled air.

"I don't savvy it, Smith. The *Constantine's* cargo is consigned to me."

"Yes; but I have a quarter interest in the firm, therefore in that cargo. I'll make it over to you for nothing, as agreed, and—"

"Look here!" exploded Ward. "You're buying a quarter interest in this business, and paying by means of your interest in the next cargo to arrive—what the devil! Do you think you can get away with such a technicality? You can't buy into my firm, using my own goods! It's absolutely illegal!"

"No law here, no courts," said Smith. His blue eyes were dancing; those of Ward were angry. "I'm a partner as of this date, remember; naturally my interest includes this incoming cargo."

"Like hell it does!" snapped Ward. "You can't put over any such slick trick on me!"

Smith chuckled. "It's put, ain't it?"

"You knew all the time it was my ship that was coming!"

"Sure," agreed Smith placidly. "I'm buying half her cargo from you, remember."

Ward choked wrathfully. Then he lost his temper and stormed; Smith ignored his profane threats and open fury, and glanced at the papers, and nodded.

"I'll have close to ten thousand hides for you," he observed.

"And seventy hogsheads of tallow, remember. At a neat five per cent discount. That means money."

Ward flew into a fury and damned the hides and tallow.

Smith remained calm. "I can ship it, if you don't want it. But there'll be a fat profit there for the firm, partner. On top of that, your ten per cent profit from the sale of half your cargo to me. I've already arranged a resale."

"To whom?" demanded Ward, who had never thought of such a possibility.

"Captain Leidesdorff."

"What?" Ward's fury mounted. "That damned pirate? I wouldn't sell a barrel of codfish to that rascal at any price!"

"You're not. I am," said Smith quietly. "And you can't stop me."

This was obvious, even to Ward, and heightened his rage.

"You cursed smart Yankee, that agreement isn't worth the paper it's written on!" he stormed. "Buying into my business, with my own property—it's a trick, and nothing more, a cheap Yankee trick! It doesn't have a shadow of justice or right, not a shadow!"

"I know it," said Abel Smith. Ward's anger was checked; he sat staring.

"You know it?"

"Sure. I never expected to take advantage of it; I don't now," said Smith, smiling slightly. "Tear up that agreement if you like. You see, Ward, there'd be no value in a partnership gained by fraud and trickery, would there? The gain lies in making you see that you do need a cute partner around to protect mutual interests; such a partner would be invaluable to you. There are a lot of smart people around here, and two men hanging together could outsmart 'em all—easier than one could."

"My lord! Are you in earnest?" gasped Ward.

"Dead earnest. That's why I had you agree to that other clause, about buying the quarter interest outright. That's why I put myself in your hands, bound myself to pay any amount you might name. Go on and name it. I'll pay it. I'm profiting from these deals and can well afford to do so. I like you. I think this town may have a future; we could travel far and fast with it, if we had a mind. It isn't much of a place right now, but it may grow. Some think it's bound to grow. You and I together might go to work on a lot of ideas that are crowding me."

The twinkling blue eyes had become steady. Smith spoke with slow, earnest argument and meant his words. His bony features were intent and resolute. Ward watched him and the angry, eyes quieted, finding in the steady blue ones an almost wistful appeal.

"What d'you say?" concluded Smith. "Nantucket and New York might make an awfully good team, Ward, if they'd pull together."

Frank Ward stood up. His hard, set face relaxed.

"I'd suggest," he replied, "that we go have a drink, and then get supper—as arranged. After all, we shook hands on the bargain, didn't we? Let's keep it."

"Fine!" Abel Smith sighed and rose. "We'll step around to John Henry's bar, and for once I'll forget my principles. Just once. It's been a long day. By the way, when will the sign be painted?"

"It'll be finished and hung next Wednesday," said Ward, grinning suddenly. "Suit you?"

"Oh, yes," said Abel Smith. It suited him excellently. Leidesdorff was leaving on the morrow and would not be back for a week or ten days. Time enough to meet that hurricane when it blew up. The captain was going to be disturbed, and more than disturbed, when he saw the sign announcing the new firm.

11

THE CAPTAIN HAS ENEMIES

Yerba Buena Was a Village of Exiled
Men, and Gossip Was Its Life

THE JUNIOR partner of Ward & Smith was getting a dressing-down out in front of his own store, and all Yerba Buena was hastening to the scene in high glee.

Captain Leidesdorff, just back from a trip to Sutter's fort, had discovered that Abel Smith, instead of taking a job from him, was teamed up with a rival merchant. Aside from being the most prominent and colorful citizen in town, the ex-sea captain had a very remarkable temper and vocabulary, and when he really let himself go in his stentorian quarterdeck voice, he could be heard over on the Contra Costa shores.

Smith stood silent and miserable, a pilloried victim, too proud to duck back into the store but unable to get in a word endways. His bony features were flushed; his Adam's apple bobbed at each fresh epithet, his bright blue eyes flickered appealing at the throng, and found only grins.

"You're an ingrate," thundered Leidesdorff in a quotable moment. "You came off a ship broke and hungry and asked my help. I fed you, gave you credit, promised you a good job, and you bit the hand that fed you! Turned on me, you miserable Yankee! I helped you to make some money when you needed it worst, when you had not a dollar in your pocket—"

"Two dollars," cut in Smith, when the captain paused for breath. "Had two dollars when I came ashore, Cap'n. And I got you the cargo goods you needed...."

His words were drowned under a torrent of choice Danish,

French and English profanity as Leidesdorff found voice. The essence of vituperation, as every woman knows, is to eschew all reason or fairness or justice, and the good captain thundered on. Into the doorway of the store came Frank Ward, grinning widely, and caught his share of the fun.

"Ward & Smith—argh! I'll put the two of you out of business," roared Leidesdorff, his swarthy features darkly flushed with anger. "You and your Yankee shenanigans! You can't pull that sort of trickery in California. I'll make Yerba Buena too hot to hold you! I'll make you rue the day when my back was turned and you kicked me—"

"Who could resist such a temptation?" shouted somebody, and laughter shrilled.

The brawny captain swung around. He loved a quarrel or a fight, and was quite capable of taking on the whole crowd, but at this instant came diversion. Captain Montgomery of the *Portsmouth*, lying across at the Sausalito bight, had just landed with a liberty party, and the strapping commander pushed through the crowd and greeted Leidesdorff.

"Ha! Come along, Captain—must see you immediately— highly urgent business!"

Leidesdorff was swept away, arm in arm, unable to protest. The laughing crowd dispersed. Smith thankfully dodged into the store, met the amused gaze of his partner, and shook his head.

"It is bad for business," he observed. "We do not want enemies, especially the most important man in town and a competitor. Somehow, I must regain his good will."

"Oh, nobody minds what the captain says," replied Ward tolerantly. "He quarrels with everybody. He was sore because he had lost your services, Abel, and he was unjust too. You forget it; he'll come around. Well, see you later."

Customers began to throng in, and Smith got to work. The store, still uncompleted, was already crammed with merchandise, for a ship had come in with consignments from New York

WARD & SMITH

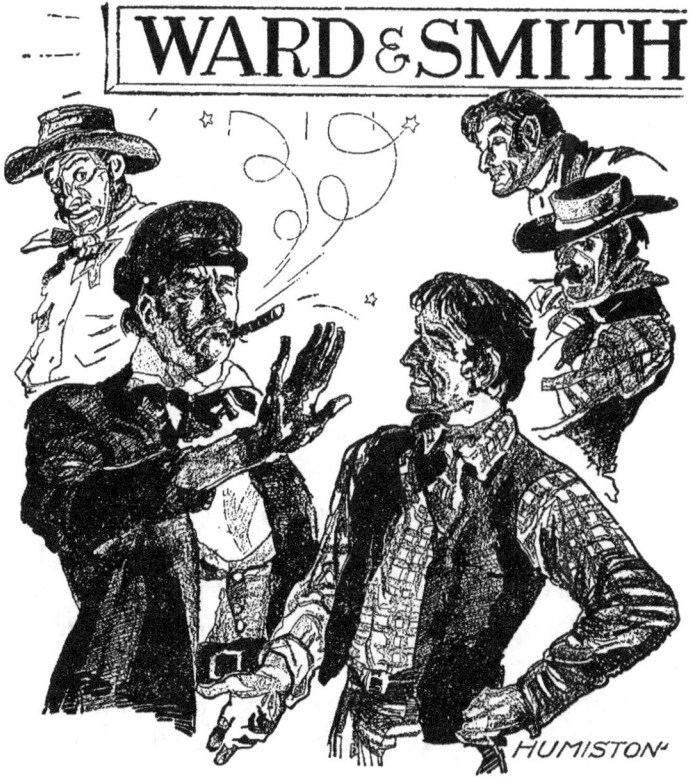

HUMISTON

and everybody in town wanted a look at the stock. The town's population was well over a hundred, and more pouring in. It was the end of September, '46. The Oregon rush was on full force, and wagon-trains were beginning to troop into California, annexed to the United States in July. It was the shipping that helped Yerba Buena, however—traders from the Islands, whalers, sturdy Cape Horners from Boston and Salem, occasional warships.

SMITH, BUSTLING around, kept his ears open. The crowd, in the main, was young; only young men picked this new country for settlement. There was O'Farrell, in his early twenties, a genial Irishman seeking his fortune and needing a pair of shoes at the moment; talking with him was a dandified figure that drew Smith's gaze.

Sam Brannan, of course—everybody knew him.

He had come out in charge of the Mormon ship in July, had fought with his charges, and when the Mormon emigration found itself unable to colonize here, had stayed on in Yerba Buena. Dandified, bombastic, with dead black sideburns and imperial, Brannan had adventured all over the country—he was only twenty-six now.

At an ebb in the rush, O'Farrell caught Smith's eye and beckoned.

"Shoes! Brogans!" he exclaimed. "Get out your best on credit, Abel. Shake hands with Sam Brannan—Smith's a particular friend of mine, Sam. And of Captain Leidesdorff."

"Yes, I heard the cap'n saying so," said Brannan, chuckling as he shook hands. "Glad to meet you."

"Smith landed with two dollars and inside of twenty-four hours was in business," said O'Farrell. "Beats your record, Sam. Is it true that when your ship got in and found the American flag flying and your chances at filibustering all gone, you swore?"

"No. I never swear," said Brannan, his black eyes all alive. "I remember saying that there was that damned flag again—we couldn't get away from it! Hey, Smith! Know anything about flour mills?"

"Used to work in one when I was a boy," said Smith, bundling out shoe samples.

"Ask him anything you want to know, Sam," O'Farrell said. "He knows everything and can do anything, but he's a green-horn in California. Time he's been here three months, he'll own the place. Here we are, Abel. Just what I want. Now for the right size. You can trust Sam like you would my own self—just within sight. Remember, he's a Mormon, but he's a bad one so that makes it all right."

O'Farrell joked himself into his new shoes, signed a credit slip, and was off. Sam Brannan remained, and beckoned Abel Smith into a corner.

"My friend, you're a Yankee; so am I. Born in Maine and

been traveling ever since. I've got a house in that street on the edge of town—Clay Street, they call it. And within those walls are imprisoned the whole future greatness and glory, even the daily bread, of Yerba Buena and perhaps of all California!"

Smith enjoyed the hypnotic spell of the man, because he could resist it easily.

"Is that a joke, Mr. Brannan?" he asked. The other grunted.

"No, dammit! I've got a printing press there; I'm a printer. I intend to publish a newspaper, but it's impossible to get any paper, in this primitive land. Further, I have two flour mills— two! The only two in California. Mexicans use unbolted, coarse flour that's unfit for human consumption. They were taken apart for shipment and I can't get 'em put together. Imprimis, I need a mechanical genius to do it. Secundis—or should it be secundum?—is the question of grain to make into flour. Nobody does any farming in this country except John Sutter, over on the Sacramento. Can Ward & Smith afford any help in my two problems?"

Smith reflected briefly. This flour business was important; tortillas were all right for Californians, but Americans cursed them bitterly and longed in vain for bread that was bread. It might be a big thing.

"Ward & Smith can do anything," he replied cheerfully, "if you just give 'em time, Mr. Brannan."

"Say that again!" declaimed the other. "Mister! You're the first person to Mister me since I've been here! Call me Sam and be damned to you, friend."

Smith grinned faintly, and his blue eyes sparkled. It was a nice sparkle; men took to him at once because of it.

"I'll come over after supper and help with the mills," he said. "Might as well put in my evenings doing something useful and it's mighty crowded sleeping in the back room of the store with the lumber and paint."

"Don't," said Brannan warningly. "Mighty unhealthy. I'll put you up in my adobe mansion. My wife's a splendid cook; come to supper, remain to work, and quit work to sleep. That way we can work later at the blasted machinery."

"Are you really a printer?" asked Abel Smith. Brannan rolled his eyes to heaven.

"Am I? In Ohio, New Orleans and Indiana, the name of Brannan is renowned as that of a master printer who failed but conquered all type lice. Did you never hear of that noble journal, the Messenger of the Latter Day Saints? My handiwork, friend; presiding elder Sam Brannan, owner, editor, publisher, printer! Come to the house promptly at seven and bring your nightgown and toothbrush, and expect comfort but no palatial quarters."

Smith, by this time, figured Brannan as half jocular and altogether charming; a true estimate. He was not refined in language, but this was a very minor detail in Yerba Buena. For the rest of the day, Abel Smith went about very cheerfully at the prospect of having found a home—also, a problem or two upon which to exercise his wits. He hoped the day would end better than it had begun. Thought of Leidesdorff's threats still bothered him.

ABEL SMITH liked this hamlet at the end of the world. He had ever been productive of ideas in huge variety, always amounting to nothing; but the salt-scented, fog-fresh air of Yerba Buena seemed to stimulate his notions in a rushing stream. Everything he saw or heard suggested something to him. Within the past ten days he had fairly staggered Frank Ward with his conception of how the business should run and be expanded; and being himself in his early twenties, and enthusiastic, Ward put most of them into practice and found them shrewdly good. He laughed at the Yankee from Nantucket, but admired him.

That same afternoon, for instance, O'Farrell dropped into the store to make some purchases. He was going to Sonoma on the morrow, where he had a small ranch, and needed gifts for the Vallejo family. Don Mariano Vallejo was the greatest man in the north and the chief Californian, owning vast quantities of land about Sonoma. While O'Farrell bought—on credit as usual—he talked in his nimble way of whatever came into his mind.

"Your friend Leidesdorff has a new and a vital worry," he told Smith, laughingly. "You know, he's banking heavily on Yerba Buena as the coming metropolis of the country. Well, Larkin down at Monterey, who's practically a millionaire already and the sharpest trader in California, is going in with Vallejo to start a new town up north, across the bay. They're going to do it on a big scale, too."

"How will that affect the captain?" Smith demanded.

"Because they're going to name it Francisca, after Don Mariano's wife—and everyone in the east knows of San Francisco Bay, and nobody ever heard of Yerba Buena—and Larkin is sending pieces about it to all the eastern newspapers. Savvy?" O'Farrell broke into a laugh. "It'll put Yerba Buena out of business, certain! In fact, I'm going up there now to see how things shape up. I may transfer all my interests there. Others may do the same. Larkin's got a powerful big name around here, for a fact! How d'you like Brannan?"

"Oh! Nice fellow," said Smith. "I'm going to help him put his machinery together."

"Watch out for him—he's a dreamer, and can talk you out of your right arm!" said O'Farrell, with a chuckle. "Still, he has money, I hear; he's already bought a ranch up the Stanislaus River. Sometimes these dreamers get somewhere."

This talk left Abel Smith thoughtful. Half a dozen ideas popped up in his head, each heading in a different direction, and he forced them back; he knew that he must stick to practical things. Frank Ward had warned him about that; Ward was a bit worried lest the Yankee genius get him into difficulties. And he knew Ward was right.

Still that new town sounded promising. He went to Ward about it, mentioning that the firm might do worse than get in on the ground floor up there, without competition.

"Without competition?" Ward laughed scornfully. "Listen! Larkin has a finger in half the enterprises going. Jacob Leese, at Sonoma, runs the store there; he's Vallejo's brother-in-law, get it? Those three make a combination nobody could beat. This new town, Francisca—do you think Leese would let another firm in on the ground floor? Only in a coffin, my friend—and they'd have to buy the coffin from Leese!"

"I see," murmured Smith, disturbed. "I didn't understand."

"You'd better understand a lot of things, before you jump Ward & Smith into any such hot water. Oh, I know it was just an idea," Ward added, in his kindly way, "and no harm done. Forget it. Look, there's that old Californian coming back—see what he wants, will you? I can't savvy a word he says, and he doesn't talk English."

Smith hurried off toward a gray-mustached, heavy-set man at the front of the store, whose serape proclaimed him a Californian.

It was typical of Abel Smith that, while working his way on a Nantucket whaler out to California, he had assiduously picked up a kind of Spanish from a Cape Verde boatsteerer. It was as bad as the equally mangled Spanish spoken by the Californians, but it permitted Smith to get along with the latter.

So he chattered away with the old chap, who was down from San Rafael on a shopping expedition. They talked at some length, and it turned out that the old fellow owned a ranch of something like forty thousand acres, which Smith could not quite believe. The old one was highly delighted with Smith's brand of Spanish, and with Smith himself, and they had a lengthy discussion about where grain could be procured to make flour.

It may be that Mr. Smith, far from comprehending that the old boy was actually a Don with a capital D, and in Californian eyes a personage, committed himself just a thought too eagerly. Nor did he precisely understand that the local term *fanega* meant not a bushel, but more than two bushels, of wheat. In fact, Smith did not pay much attention to the conversation, and presently forgot it entirely.

SUPPER AT Sam Brannan's was an event; work on the machinery was interesting; the ensuing bed, to replace his hard pallet in the back room of the store, was delightful. Now, from early morn to late at night, Abel Smith really labored. Those few days were big ones, and Yerba Buena was roaring from dawn to dusk; the frigate *Congress,* bearing Commodore Stockton, dropped anchor in the bay. So did a French warship. So did a ship from the islands, bearing Mr. Grimes of Honolulu and other notables. Yerba Buena promptly went into fiesta, and a fiesta in Yerba Buena had no sober connotations.

Abel Smith was only vaguely aware of these extraneous events. Once he met Leidesdorff and O'Farrell, returned from Sonoma; both were very amiable and very drunk.

ONCE HE met the burly captain when sober, and received a black look and an oath. He was too busy even to care about this. He was, with Brannan, getting those two flour mills in shape.

"But what the devil good is it going to do me?" Brannan said gloomily, one evening after supper. "There's no wheat to be had. Sutter grows some, not enough to sell. A good many settlers are beginning to grow it—only beginning."

"Have you looked around?" queried Smith. "Don't the Californians grow it?"

Sam Brannan grimaced. "I heard a rumor to that effect— Vallejo does, I believe. I tried to run it down. No luck! Can't make 'em sell to me, or even admit having wheat. They trade with their own people, blast 'em! There's no money in grinding flour for other people. I want to grind my own and make money on the sale."

"There should be good profit in it," Smith said thoughtfully.

"Don't I know it? Those ships—why, that frigate in the bay is crying for flour, and not a sack to be had! Everybody's hollering for bread, dammit, and I can't work a miracle and turn stones into bread."

"Maybe you've fallen from grace, that's why," said Smith. Brannan gave him a sharp look, met the twinkling eyes, and went into a gale of laughter.

The mills were completed and ready.

Now, Yerba Buena was a village of exiled men, and gossip was its life. Everyone knew the most intimate details about everybody else; especially in a business way did rumor thrive and reach afar. This was not a matter to be taken lightly, but it was a fact to which Smith paid scant heed.

He had overworked; so definitely so that Frank Ward took him in hand one fine morning and brought him up with a round jerk.

"Pack up, Abel. You're going to Sutter's fort. Sutter's launch leaves at noon."

"I'm—what?" demanded Smith blankly. Ward nodded at him, and handed him a letter.

"Here's a note from Sutter. He wants a large order; it's going aboard his launch now. You're going with it. Sutter's credit is definitely bad; he owes thirty thousand in one quarter alone, he owes Leidesdorff immense sums, he owes everybody! It's important that we don't lose out, yet we mustn't anger Sutter— he has influence. He's a nice old chap, sort of baronial, and under the surface I suspect he has no more scruples than a Yankee. You handle him. Can you get away?"

"Why, I guess so! It'll put all the work on you—"

"I'll take care of that," said Ward. "It's a three-day trip, sometimes four; you'll be back in a week or over, and the change will do you good. Luck to you!" He broke into a laugh, and added: "I hear Leidesdorff went up there yesterday in his own launch. If you run into him, don't start a fight."

Before he realized it was all true, Abel Smith was aboard the fifty-ton craft—in Yerba Buena parlance, a launch—along with piles of freight, half a dozen passengers and three swarthy, merry Californians who served as crew.

I T WA S like a dream trip to him; the sail up the wide bay to the narrows, through the Carquinez Straits, on through to the Sacremento—camping at night, pushing on by day—the Sacramento itself, little less than a mile wide—he had not dreamed of such a country, with its hills and far white peaks and lavish forests, with scarcely the smoke of a hunter's fire to be seen anywhere.

Then the fort and the embarcadero, and his first indications of the war between the States and Mexico, so lightly and distantly regarded at Yerba Buena. Soldiers here, guards and cannon at the bastions, an officer of the *Portsmouth* in command, and bustly, hearty John Sutter, no longer master of his own house and sadly aware of it. Hunters, Indian fighters—and Leidesdorff. Smith ran into him that first night at dinner.

To his surprise, Leidesdorff nodded amiably to him and even handed him a cigar.

"Well! I'm glad you're feeling better about everything, Captain," said Smith.

"I'm not, young man. I'm feeling worse. But here we're away from home and we should be at truce."

"Fine," said Smith cheerfully. "Sometime when you feel like it, I'd be glad of a talk with you. I really do appreciate all you did for me. I'd like to help you with your own problems, and believe I can do it."

"You? Help me?" Leidesdorff purpled and his voice became a roar. "My problems?"

"Yes. About this town they're going to build up the bay, to knock Yerba Buena into a cocked hat, as they call it—"

"Be damned to your impudence!" bellowed Leidesdorff, then checked himself and would say no more, but turned his back.

Smith was hurt. He had a real liking, even an affection, for the brawny captain, and this evidence of renewed anger left him dismayed. He did not see Leidesdorff again, as the captain left early in the morning with his own boat.

That day Smith accomplished his business with Sutter, while the launch was emptied and laden again for the return trip, with great bales of hides for export and barrels of salt salmon. Sutter was friendly, paternal in his urbane way; he knew exactly why Smith had come along and made things easy for him, being acutely aware of his own tremendous debts.

He had little with which to pay, but rustled up various accounts payable of his own and made them over to Ward & Smith. Then:

"If you'd like the balance in wheat, I could give you that at once," he said. "I could send it down by next week's launch—at two dollars fifty a *fanega,* it would just balance our account. I'd make you a good discount on the price, of course."

Smith thought fast. Wheat! Just what San Brannan most wanted and would pay well to have!

"It's a deal," he said. "What made you think I'd want wheat?"

"Oh," replied Sutter in his Germanic accent, "Captain Leidesdorff mentioned that your firm was trying to get some wheat."

Abel Smith was astonished, even puzzled, but regarded it as of no consequence; this was a stroke of luck, indeed. So he made all square with Sutter on behalf of Ward & Smith, and departed next morning with the launch, quite happily.

The down trip ran into adverse tides at the river sloughs and took a day longer than the trip up, but Smith enjoyed every minute of the open air life. He felt, and was, like a new man. His bony features had lost their haggard look, his bright blue eyes had taken on their old sparkle, and he saw wonders on every hand—wonders of nature and opportunity, advantages for the taking and using. A magnificent country, this California!

The last day was a short run, the launch heading in for the Yerba Buena cove about noon. As soon as he set foot ashore,

Smith hurried up the sandy street to the store and was astonished to find Ward just closing the doors.

"Heard the launch was coming," said Ward. His manner was
strange. "Come on in. We must have a talk at once."

"Anything wrong?" demanded Smith. Ward's features were
chill and set.

"Don't know yet," came the curt reply.

Being hungry, Smith helped himself to some crackers and
cheese, then joined Ward in the office at the rear of the store.
Ward's manner was certainly singular.

"Have a nice trip?" he asked.

"Glorious! And I've got everything cleaned up with Sutter,
too. Took his bills payable to half the amount due, and a thousand bushels of wheat for the balance. Do you know, he has a
wheat crop this year of over six thousand bushels?"

Ward made a queer sound in his throat, and forced a smile
that was a grimace.

"That's fine, fine!" he said bitterly. "More wheat! Now, Abel,
some things have happened while you were gone. First, do you
know a Californian named Don Miguel de Rosa, who has a
land grant up north?"

"Rosa? No. I've heard the name, I think," said Smith, frowning. "Why?"

"Reason enough, my worthy partner. What I've been afraid
of, has taken place. It seems that this Don Miguel was in the
store one day and had a long conversation with you about wheat.
Think hard. Can't you remember it?"

Smith stared at his partner wonderingly. "Hm! There was an
old gray-mustached fellow wearing a dirty serape—remember,
you couldn't savvy his lingo and I waited on him?

"Yes, seems to me we did talk about wheat, and how hard it
was to pick up any. Sam Brannan could use a lot of it."

WARD EXPLODED, cuttingly, "Hard to pick up any!
Well, Don Miguel has picked some up for you. He's picked

some up from Vallejo, from everybody up north who was growing it. Leidesdorff heard of it and has helped him greatly. The mission buildings at San Rafael, where old Murphy has charge, are bursting with wheat consigned to you. The sheds at Sausalito are filled. As near as I can discover, there are about ten thousand *fanegas* of this excellent wheat, all consigned to Ward & Smith, waiting to come across the bay."

"Ten thousand! And I have a thousand bushels more coming from Sutter!" Smith gaped for a moment, then broke into a laugh. "Why, that's splendid, Frank! What makes you think it isn't?"

"My perverted sense of values, no doubt," said .Ward with angry sarcasm. "Who's going to pay for this wheat, at two dollars fifty per *fanega? A fanega* is over two bushels, mind."

"Oh, that's all right," Smith replied confidently. "You don't understand. We'll make a good profit on it. Ordinary unbolted, coarse flour, like Sutter turns out in his horse mill, brings eight dollars a hundred pounds. Fine bolted American flour will bring even more. We can take all the wheat we can use."

"Indeed? Speak for yourself; it's your idea. Now, listen, my fine Yankee partner! Leidesdorff has got us where he wants us. Ordinarily, that wheat could be shipped to the Islands. I spoke to Grimes about it—he's here from Honolulu on a visit. The old rat grinned and said sure, take it all over to Grimes & Davis, and they'd pay us a dollar and a half per *fanega.* He let the cat out of the bag. We're stuck, understand?"

Smith, perceiving the possibilities, lost his cheerful air.

"I don't see why," he said stubbornly. "People have to eat. Ships need flour. My idea is to sell all the wheat we can get to Sam Brannan. His two flour mills are waiting for it—"

"Your idea! Sam Brannan!" shot out Ward in cold anger. "You and that windbag between you have ruined Ward & Smith, that's what! If we don't take these consignments, our credit in this country is finished. If we take it, we're finished—drowning in wheat we can't use or sell, except at a handsome loss! Stifled in it! Choked in it!"

"Frank, you've jumped off before looking," argued Smith earnestly. "I think Don Miguel or whoever he is, misunderstood me; anyhow, he acted as a friend, and the firm needs all the good will it can get among these Californians."

"We've certainly got it, and they'll get our money," snapped Ward.

"That's all right. I'll go over and see Brannan, and everything will be fine."

Ward's gaze was piercing and chill. "Is it your optimistic notion that Sam Brannan will take this wheat off our hands?"

"I know he will. It's the very thing he wants most."

"Brannan's credit isn't good for a dollar," said Ward. "Go see him and find out."

Hunger forgotten, Abel Smith lost no time in doing just that. His first dismay had passed into anxiety, which became more acute as he recalled Leidesdorff's manner at Sutter's fort. Even kindly old Sutter had been in the plot, saddling him with another thousand bushels. However, he still had confidence that Frank Ward had leaped at conclusions.

He found the Brannans at table and was eagerly welcomed. It was hard not to blurt out everything; but he managed to contain himself. As usual, Brannan was charming and bombastic, full of airy schemes, absolutely positive of their practical value—and, rather surprisingly, correct about it. Smith found himself reassured by the splendid presence, and when the meal was over, followed quite cheerfully to another room where they could talk in private. Brannan had a dozen irons in the fire and was enthusiastic about them all.

"I've got a lease on a fine redwood house back of the Old Adobe," he said. "At least, it's a house that'll do. I'm going to install the printing outfit there—well, I see you have something on your mind, so fire away."

Abel Smith lost no time about it, going into full detail. As he went on talking, his heart began to sink. Brannan looked worried, fingering his goatee, losing his confident manner, his black eyes plucking at the air around.

"So there's the situation," Smith concluded. "There's a lot of money, or credit, involved. I knew you were trying to get wheat, and now we've enough and to spare."

"Yes, yes," said Brannan. "And to spare—that's right. And it's a lot of money, dammit! Well, Abel, let's get down to brass tacks. I can't take over your wheat."

Smith swallowed hard. "You can't?"

"Not that I wouldn't like to—why, it's what I've been dreaming about! But just now I'm in a bad pinch. That ranch I bought on the Stanislaus has me nipped. Then, the Mormon company breaking up has left me high and dry for the moment. You see, we were all confident that this was the place to colonize. Brigham Young started across country, I came by sea. Now Young has found a paradise near the Salt Lake and is settling there, calling in all the faithful—and to be honest about it, I've broken off relations with the Saints. For the moment, Abel, I'm crippled, and that's the truth. I've been trying to get credit around here and it's a tough job."

Smith's throat was dry, as his idol crumbled, and he stared at Brannan with stricken eyes. But no sooner was Brannan's confession made, than the man took fire anew.

"Look, Abel!" he exclaimed vibrantly. "I'm going to be a rich man, a millionaire; nothing can stop me! It's just for the moment. Somehow, somewhere, I'll get the bit of credit I need. I haven't lost hope by a long shot! Once I get it, we're off! Now, I can tell you how we can handle this wheat situation and block these rascals who are out to ruin you, and get our own start."

Smith relaxed. "Fine, Sam. How?"

"Instead of selling the wheat to me, which I want but can't buy, let Ward & Smith come in with me as partners on the whole deal! Think of the garrison, think of the ships in the harbor—I was aboard the *Congress* yesterday, and you should have heard them curse the coarse Mexican flour and ground corn they have to use! I could put a thousand pounds of properly milled flour aboard that one ship alone, and at a good price, too. You have the flour, I have the mills here going begging, and it's a crying shame not to take advantage of it!"

THERE WERE possibilities here; as Brannan went on to paint the glowing picture, Abel Smith's faith rekindled. Help was to be had cheaply; a dozen men working the mills, sacking the flour which the ships would gladly pick up ashore, and the thing was accomplished! Not the ships alone, either. Leidesdorff's enormous house was going to be put to use.

"Other flour mills are being imported," went on Brannan, "but we'd be first in the game and would get the cream skimmed off at high prices, before a drop comes. The set-up is perfect. Abel! Talk your partner into it."

Smith went back to the store, once more opened and running, and at the first chance took Frank Ward aside and recounted his conversation with Brannan. But Ward did not warm to it in the least.

"You've got a quarter-interest in Ward & Smith, Abel," he rejoined. "With the option of buying another quarter and making it a full partnership. When that day comes, I want you to realize the necessity of keeping a cool head, talking things over before you put ideas into effect, and planning with your partner."

It was the salutary wisdom of twenty-four cautioning twenty-two; but it was well meant and kindly. Ward was, however, absolutely firm about it.

"No," he said to Smith's eager pleading, "I'll have no part in the scheme at all. I think Sam Brannan is a hopeless dreamer. My advice to you is to go see Leidesdorff at once and knuckle under; he's inspiring this thing, although Don Miguel certainly acted in a friendly way."

"But it means a terrific loss!" said Smith blankly.

"I expect so. Leidesdorff's a generous soul at times, though, and if you throw yourself on his mercy, he may shave down his pound of flesh a bit. Try it, for that's your best chance. The quicker you do it, the better. Don't delay. Go now."

Abel Smith dropped everything and went, with the sickening conviction that Ward's advice was better than good.

A lump in his throat, he came into Leidesdorff's untidy emporium, and made his way toward the railed-in office, whence was issuing the well-known voice of Stentor. Jasper O'Farrell was seated there, and nodded blithely to him. Leidesdorff gave him a glare and ignored him. He waited, awkwardly uncomfortable.

The honest captain was in a bellowing fury, an ominous prelude to hopes for mercy. O'Farrell was all agog with the plans of Don Mariano Vallejo, backed by Larkin, for the new city on the bay, to the north. Larkin was pulling out his interests in Yerba Buena, and others were doing the same—for Larkin was easily the most successful man in California, and even O'Farrell was seriously considering tailing him.

"And to think he was my best friend!" Leidesdorff's rage was spasmodic with profanity. "To think we worked and planned together! Now he stabs me in the back—for he knows that Yerba Buena means everything to me. I could forgive treachery from some young Yankee whippersnapper who knows no better," and his eye touched for an instant on Abel Smith, who shrank miserably. "But I can't forgive this action of Larkin's! Well, I stick here! My interests stick here! If you clear out and follow those rascals, you'll regret it!"

O'Farrell laughed and rose. "Oh, I have not done that yet, Captain. Well, I'll be on my way and let you roar at Smith for a change. Be seeing you!"

He swaggered away. Leidesdorff turned and scowled savagely at Smith.

"What you want here?"

"A talk with you."

"Come in. Sit down. Do your talking and clear out."

Smith took the chair vacated by O'Farrell, and swallowed hard.

"I—I—well, Cap'n, I guess I'm sunk," he said. "This business of wheat."

Leidesdorff licked his lips and regarded his visitor with grim enjoyment.

"What about it?" he demanded. "Ward & Smith can handle a little deal like that."

"Ward isn't in it. It's my affair," said Smith miserably. "And it isn't a little deal at all, for me. It's a big one. Too big."

"Talk," grunted Leidesdorff. "You were damned quick to jump at partnership with Frank Ward, when I expected you to come to work for me. Go on, talk, tell me about it."

ABEL SMITH complied. The captain knew all about it, of course, but wanted to hear him expound the details. It was something to relish, putting one of these arrogant young Easterners in his proper place, and the captain relished it.

"I'm licked, and I realize it," concluded Smith unhappily. "I'll have to get out of it the best I can, sell off that wheat at ruinous prices."

"Hm! You ain't quitting that easy?" grunted Leidesdorff with open contempt. "What about that elegant partner of yours— mean to say he won't lend you a hand?"

"He thinks I need a lesson. I guess he's right. I didn't consult him in the first place about this matter. I can't expect him to make good my losses."

"Yah!" spat out the captain. "That's a hell of a partner! You picked the wrong horse and you know it, eh?"

"No," said Smith sturdily. "He's dead right about it. I don't blame him a particle."

"Well, I do!" roared the other, "He took you away from me, blast him! He's the one I blame. Why in hell don't you and him use your wits, find some way out?"

"We did. He won't go in for it. Brannan would take us in

with him—but Frank won't have it. He's definitely out of the whole thing." The bright blue eyes were dull and hopeless, as they met those of the captain, as Smith went on to tell about Brannan's scheme in detail. "It's a good scheme and I know it," he concluded, "but Ward won't have it. All I can do is to take my licking, Cap'n, and get out with as little loss as possible."

"That's what anybody has to do who goes up against me," said Leidesdorff, taking a fresh cigar and champing at it with obvious satisfaction. As his sharp gaze explored the bony, desperate features, the bitter hopelessness of the blue eyes, his swarthy features softened curiously but his voice remained harsh and leonine.

"Yes, sir, old Leidesdorff has claws, and he can use 'em!" he went on savagely. "Any of you people who think he's soft, will learn better. Larkin—damn his eyes!—will learn better one of these days. Big man, founding cities, wrecking other places, is he? I'll teach him how big he is! Bob Ridkey's behind the bars now because he double-crossed old Leidesdorff, and Larkin will go the same way or worse. Him and his new city—arrgh!"

SMITH LOOKED up suddenly. "You know, sir, how you could knock his whole scheme in the head? I told you at Sutter's fort there was a way."

"Ha! So you did. More of your fine Yankee notions, eh? How?"

"Why, sir, like this. This bay is known everywhere as San Francisco Bay, isn't it? Nobody ever heard of Yerba Buena. His new city will be named Francisca, to take advantage of that, and all the people who are coming will head for there. Well, sir, you're the most influential man here in Yerba Buena—why don't you get the town's name changed to that of the bay—San Francisco? That would settle him, turn the tables on him—why, what's the matter?"

Leidesdorff stared at him, motionless yet in singular motion. The fierce eyes dilated and bulged; a tide of color suffused the swarthy features darkly. The thick lips compressed and tightened. Slowly, Leidesdorff laid down his cigar, and started breathing, heavily.

"Holy—holy smoke!" he rumbled. "San Francisco! As I live and breathe—why, damn your perishing eyes! Young man, you've hit it! You've hit it!"

"Oh! Then you like the idea?" exclaimed Smith in delight.

"Like it! Why, it—it's magnificent!" he declared, when the first steam had blown off. He reached out, seized a handful of cigars, and thrust them at Smith. "Here, smoke up! We are friends. Old Leidesdorff knows a good friend when he sees one, young man. Now—I tell you what to do, about this wheat business. Come back to that for a minute. So Frank Ward won't touch it, eh?"

"No. He definitely won't."

"Good! Then you go ahead with Sam Brannan. I know him; he's no fraud. Go ahead with him! Make flour and sell it!"

"But—Captain! You don't understand!" cried Smith, dazedly. "I can't do that, I can't handle all this wheat—I've no credit of my own—"

"Young man, when you have old Leidesdorff behind you, there's nothing you can't do—nothing!" The captain's fist slammed down on the desk. "Go ahead! I'll back your credit without limit! And listen—one thing, one important thing!" Leidesdorff leaned forward and took Smith's lapel in his big fingers. His voice dropped, really dropped, to a veritable whisper.

"Don't say anything—not a word to a soul—about this idea—about San Francisco!" he breathed. "Understand? Not a word! If that damned Larkin got hold of it, he'd jump at it. I'll do what's necessary—I'll do it myself—I'll knock his damned new city into a cocked hat. San Francisco—oh, it's beautiful, beautiful!"

When Abel Smith sought the street again, his blue eyes were sparkling eagerly, and he was hurrying so fast that he almost fell over himself, getting somewhere.

III

GENTLEMAN'S AGREEMENT

*A Yankee Trader Learns of Business as
Done in Early California—Between
Caballeros and Gentlemen*

A BEL SMITH, pockets heavy with the quail which he had trapped—they were abundant in the bush around the village—stood looking thoughtfully down at the little cove. The tents and haphazard buildings ran down to the beach from the plaza—now grandly named Portsmouth Square, from the sloop of war which had hoisted the Stars and Stripes here in July. The tide was out at the moment, and the cove was a flat of glistening mud.

To the young man from Nantucket this was now home; he was part of it, he liked it. Between his own aspect and that of Yerba Buena was a certain similarity, though he was but twenty-two and the village far older.

Both were raw-boned, awkward, earnest and resolute; the blue waters of the bay matched the sparkling blue of Abel Smith's eyes, the shore rocks were like the bony lines of his face, the stores and warehouses were like his plunder-crammed pockets. Neither old town nor young man were pretty, but both were vigorous, with room to grow.

Between its boundary ravines the village boasted more than fifty sprawling houses—a dilapidated windmill, within whose adobe walls Sam Brannan had housed his printing plant, as yet unused for lack of paper; another house occupied by the Brannan family and flour mills; a ship's deck-house, now a mansion, saloons and warehouses and stores, all of one story,

all of adobe except an occasional frame structure or a shack put together with odd planks and weathered bullock hides.

On the staff in the plaza flew the Stars and Stripes, and before it, along the old adobe custom-house, paced a solitary marine from the *Portsmouth*. The population was growing fast. Before this fall of 1846 passed into winter, there would be two hundred souls in town, or so ran optimistic hopes.

Smith wished he had been here then; with the new flag things had changed, competition was keen. True, he was now junior partner of Ward & Smith, general merchants, and his

Yankee notions were making Frank Ward step around; but in the old lazy days it had been pretty soft for a smart man around here. Look at Leidesdorff, the former sea-captain!

Leidesdorff, with his huge gusto, had got in on the ground floor. Now he was the most prominent citizen in Yerba Buena, his store and hotel and billiard-room the biggest building in town. Yet by Yerba Buena standards he was an old man—all of thirty-four. And yonder at the edge of the village lay Vioget's little ranch. A French gentleman, a musician, Vioget fiddled while Yerba Buena throve, but his saloon and billiard room throve also.

Smith glanced at the ships anchored down the expanse of the vast harbor, at the islands where clouds of Canada geese and gulls were circling, and started again for Sam Brannan's house, where he was lodging. He sighted an approaching figure and recognized a man lately arrived from the Sacramento country, Sullivan by name, a burly, serious fellow who had frequently been in the store.

"Hi, Mr. Sullivan!" he cried cheerfully. "What brings you into the sandhills this fine Sunday afternoon? Looking for quail?"

"Nope. Gathering wild mint for tea." Sullivan displayed a cluster of the trailing vine that had given Yerba Buena its name of Good Herb. "Say! I'd like to ask you something."

"Ask ahead," said Smith, tucking tobacco into his pipe carefully.

"I've got a job at the grist mill in the old adobe, where they turn out cracked wheat. It's terrible stuff, makes the worst bread a man ever sank his teeth into. They tell me Sam Brannan is making real American flour at the mills he fetched around the Horn in that Mormon ship he came in."

"Sure making good flour," Smith said cheerfully. He might well be cheerful, since he was in with Brannan on the business and doing handsomely.

"Well, it's a terrible job packing wheat and flour and store goods from the beach up to the stores, and back again," said

Sullivan. "All hand work. I been doing it. Why wouldn't a horse and wagon be better?"

Smith laughed, but something clicked in his brain and the laugh died.

Why not, indeed? Yerba Buena had no wharf, though Leides-dorff talked of building one. Loading and unloading goods and getting them up from the beach was a back-breaking job; the majority of all arrivals were by water. There was a Mexican oxcart at the mission, two and a half miles down the shore, with slab wheels, but no one would use it, or could.

"Sounds all right," he rejoined. "But where would you get a wagon?"

"They got some emigrant wagons stored up at Sutter's fort," Sullivan said. "I seen 'em when I come through. Some all took to pieces. Others they use around there. And I can get a team of horses at fifteen dollars each, and break 'em in to harness."

Smith nodded. His eyes lit up. Something worth while here—he was not sure just what, but he recognized the symp-toms of an idea.

"Look, Sullivan," he said. "Cast your eye around and make sure about those horses, and don't say why you want 'em. Sutter's in town, and I'll see him about those wagons at his place. Nobody uses wagons in California, and we might get them cheap if he didn't suspect why we want them. Drop in and see me in a couple days."

"Fine, Mr. Smith!" said Sullivan. "I'll keep a close mouth, you bet!"

Abel Smith went on home, turned over his quail to Mrs. Brannan to cook for supper, and sat down to think things out. There was a connection, but he could not place it.

The only road into Yerba Buena came up the peninsula from Santa Clara and San Jose Pueblo to the south. All the settle-ments and ranches about the enormous San Francisco bay were placed with a view to water traffic. Hides and tallow, the chief exports, came in by water; only last week Smith had persuaded

Frank Ward to buy a small launch that could pick up hides at various points about the bay. Wagons were unknown, ox-carts were ineffectual, pack-horses or mules could carry only small loads.

Sutter's fort away up the Sacramento was where any immigrants from across the plains arrived, and they were coming in, and more were coming from the east. Abel Smith puffed at his pipe and tried to recollect something; something connected with Kanaka Davis and his partner Grimes, the Honolulu traders who had a big store here, run by Davis. It eluded him.

He went out, at last, and strolled about town, trying to pin down the memory. Near the beach, he saw a figure in serape and wide hat standing beside a drawn-up boat. It was his friend Don Miguel de Rosa, who had a big land grant up near San Rafael. Don Miguel had taken a liking to the young Yaqui who spoke a queer sort of Spanish, and had helped him get wheat for Sam Brannan's flour mills. Swarthy, gray-mustached, stocky, Don Miguel did not look like a lord of many broad square miles; but he was.

"Well, what are you doing here on the shore?" said Smith, shaking hands with him.

"Waiting, señor, waiting. We have come across by boat, my brother and I, and I am going to visit him at his ranch down the bay, where the sun is warm and there is no fog."

"There's plenty here," said Smith, with a laugh.

They talked; Don Miguel spoke of his brother's broad acres, fifteen miles or so down the bay shore, and swung his hand about vaguely.

"The mission, the old buildings here, the adobe and tile—all come from down there. Once they used to make much tile in the furnace, many adobes; now there is not much demand, everybody is too busy to carry some adobe in a boat."

"Tiles, eh?" said Smith. "And adobe bricks—ah, that's it,

bricks! Don Miguel, has your brother many bricks on hand now?"

"Many? *Por Dios,* yes!" said Don Miguel, a smile breaking through his ragged gray mustache. "They must dry in the sun for two months. They are all over the ground, and no one will carry them away—they are too heavy for *carretas,* and boats cannot carry many. It is a problem, señor."

Abel Smith's blue eyes danced. "When will your brother come to Yerba Buena again?

Don Miguel shrugged. "*Quién sabe?* Perhaps when I return home, on Monday next."

"Will you ask him to see me? It might be possible to make a good sale of his adobe bricks. I am not sure."

The other agreed gravely, and Abel Smith went home to dine on quail, with thoughts buzzing in his head and ideas still vague but gradually assuming form. Bricks, Kanaka Davis, Captain Leidesdorff, and Sullivan, all somehow tangled together, and clarity not arrived.

JASPER O'FARRELL dropped in that evening. The genial Irishman had worked for Sutter originally, but was now turning his hand to a bit of everything and had some land up north near Sonoma. He roved about rather aimlessly, but managed to prosper. Just now he had a small sack of the gristmill wheat that was the California staple, and wanted some samples of real flour from Sam Brannan's mills, by way of a hideous comparison.

"If I can't sell a hundred barrels of your flour to the American settlers up that way, I'm a Dutchman!" said he gaily. "What's in it for me? Come on, me lad, talk!"

Brannan talked. In the course of the discussion, O'Farrell mentioned that Sutter was at Leidesdorff's house, and those two inveterate feasters had been at a gargantuan dinner most of the afternoon; whereupon Abel Smith took his hat and departed quietly. He had been invited to that feast, along with twenty or more other guests, and had declined; very luckily so, he now thought. Feasts were many, ideas were few.

The good captain's house was a roaring pandemonium, with everybody shouting to keep pace with stentorian Leidesdorff. Vioget fiddling away, some dancing, others singing, and Smith grinned at sight of his partner Frank Ward, the sedate New Yorker, being taught the *fandango* by Don Salvador Vallejo and his wife, in town for the occasion. Out of the wild hurly-burly, he found John Sutter seated in a corner with an officer from the *Portsmouth;* the latter, being somewhat the worse for liquor, returned to the punch-bowl and Smith took his place. He had met Sutter several times, and the genial Swiss welcomed him.

"It iss a madhouse, no?" said Sutter, beaming. "I like it. Und how iss business with Ward & Smith, my friend?"

"Not bad," said Smith modestly. "Promising, you might say. Staying with us long?"

"I must go home tomorrow." Sutter shook his head sadly. "Dose sojers, who have my fort taken over—*ach!* Here in Yerba Buena you do not know there iss a war."

"No, we just about don't, and care less, now that the American flag is up."

They chatted, Sutter pulling at a Manila cigar. He was a cherubic, pink-and-white man, with big blue eyes and a somewhat deceptive air of paternal beneficence; generous to a fault, sunk to his ears in a morass of debt, wise in tomorrow's visions but foolish in today's practical things, he ever met disillusion with his genial smile, and somehow managed to keep himself afloat and well fed to boot.

With equally deceptive Yankee frankness, Smith plunged at the mark.

"I understand, sir, that you have several emigrant's wagons at the fort, stored away."

"Ya, ya," nodded Sutter, and waved the cigar smoke from his eyes.

"They might possibly," went on Smith in his cautious way,

boyishly eager at the same time, "be traded off to a ship captain here, who is going up to Oregon and thinks they could be sold there. If he could make a little on the deal, and if I could make a little on the trade, you might get rid of them."

"Ya," repeated Sutter. "Four good vagon, my friend, four. All taken to pieces."

He reflected, and Abel Smith shrewdly let him view the situation in the round.

John August Sutter had all the wagons he could use about his own establishment; with him, they were a drug on the market, and more wagon-trains would be coming through ere long. Nobody in California wanted any wagons. The American settlers already in place would be a long time before such need developed; the California ranches used ox-carts and were content. The very idea of wagons here in San Francisco was ridiculous.

"Maybe I sell you cheap," he said at last. "It cost heavy to send them here by my launch, it cost heavy to ship to Oregon. Maybe."

"Well," said Smith, "you name a price, Cap'n Sutter."

"Dose vagon cost two hundert dollar at Independence," said the other slowly.

"New."

"Ya. New." Sutter puffed again, saw Leidesdorff bearing down on them, and spoke up. "Four vagon, one hundert dollar."

"It's a bargain," said Smith, and put out his hand. Sutter shook hands solemnly. "When can you get them here?"

"Next launch trip. Here Sunday night."

"Agreed."

Leidesdorff's bellow broke in upon them with roaring gusto and business was ended.

When the store was closing on Tuesday evening, Sullivan came in and hung about till Smith was ready to leave. They walked together to Sam Brannan's house and sat on the beach outside the door. Sullivan knew where to get the horses he wanted, down the peninsula.

"I think," said Abel Smith slowly, "that I'll have four wagons from Sutter's here, the first of next week."

"Four?" Sullivan looked startled. "But, Mr. Smith—"

"Hold on, now. They're all taken apart. You can put 'em together?"

"Sure. I know wagons. But—"

"Wait! If this town grows, Sullivan, or even if it doesn't grow, a teamster can make money. If he can have four wagons working, with greasers hired to drive the other three, he could make four times as much. Isn't that so?"

Sullivan struggled for the thought. When it dawned on him, he grinned.

"Say, you're dead right!"

"And," added Smith, "I've got a notion or two. If they work, there'd be business for all four wagons right away."

"But so many horses would be mighty expensive, and the keep besides. All that would take a lot of money."

"Prob'ly would. Suppose we go into the thing together and make a regular business of it? I'll put up the money you'll need to get started, and more as becomes necessary. You do the work and run the business. How's it strike you?"

"My land—why, it's a deal, sure enough! I'll be mighty glad."

"You keep the accounts; I'll trust you. You're the kind of man to be trusted. But be careful about one thing—don't let on to anyone here that I'm in partnership with you! Not to anyone, mind. You're doing it all yourself. Understood? Once the merchants here get used to employing a teamster to haul goods, they'll stick to it. And if the town should happen to grow, you'll have a business that may prove big in the end."

Sullivan went away awed and delighted beyond words.

E V E N I N this fall of '46, business was altogether haphazard in Yerba Buena. For example, Leidesdorff handled all the

lumber made by the steam-mill up at Bodega, and had a boat
to haul it here. Steele sold only provisions. Mellus & Howard,
who had bought out the Hudson's Bay Co. store, handled more
or less definite merchandise consignments from the East.
Grimes & Davis, did quite a business in brick, used for fire-
places and so on; it came from the Islands, also from Maine.
There was no two-story building in town except Leidesdorff's
new structure, and bricks were too expensive when adobes could
be employed at ten dollars per thousand. But out on the Pacific
shore, across the peninsula, was a small shipload of brick that
nobody could get at; and a day or two after his talk with Sullivan, Smith went over to the store of Grimes & Davis, and
had a talk with Kanaka Davis about it.

"Remember that schooner of yours," he said, "that was
wrecked on the rocks across the peninsula a couple years back?"

"Only too well," said Davis. "Her hulk is still there, washed
in among the rocks where it can't be got at with a boat. I guess
the currents have kept her from breaking up."

"Suppose I could get at her? What kind of a dicker could we
make for those brick?"

"Don't break your heart on it, young 'un," said Davis, shaking
his head. "If they could be got out, we'd have got 'em long ago.
No boat can get in among those rocks. The old schooner has
busted in two, spilling the brick all over the cove. The place it
miles away from here under high ground and just can't be got
at; if it could, there's no way of hauling the brick here."

"Will you split whatever I recover, you taking twenty per
cent?" asked Smith.

"Agreed. But I warn you, better let dead dogs lay dead and
go after live bait."

Smith looked up Sullivan that evening and told him about
the brick and the wreck.

"Unless the brick could be got out and put into a boat, it
wouldn't pay to haul it here by hand," he said. "To use a boat is
impossible. But you hire three or four greasers, and a couple of

our own kind if possible, and go over there. At low tide, that cove and hulk is exposed. Run a line, a rope, from the high shore ground down to the rocks, with a running basket. Haul the brick up and stack 'em everywhere in the grass—till we get a wagon to work. And keep quiet about it. Start the men at work, then you come back to town."

Sullivan grinned widely and went his ways. He was quick-witted enough; otherwise, he would not have been in Yerba Buena, which suffered no fools at all.

It had been customary for Frank Ward and one or two others to gather in the store of Friday evenings and have a cold snack and talk, and on this Friday evening the little gathering was honored by the presence of Leidesdorff, who contributed ale and cigars and boomed along on his favorite topic, the future greatness of Yerba Buena. It was nearly time for the rains to begin. Then the streets would be seas of mud and the world would be a dismal affair. Smith munched crackers and cheese and listened, as usual, to the talk.

"You're shouting about building more houses and ware-houses and stores, Captain," said Ward pleasantly, "but no build-ing can be done now until spring. Not with eighty-pound adobe bricks that need sunshine to dry the walls! Not to mention getting them here."

"That's true," said Leidesdorff. "It is a pity. Kanaka Davis doesn't know when a ship will come with brick. If I had only a few thousand brick, I could go ahead with my building and finish with redwood."

"What would you pay for it per thousand, Cap'n?" queried Abel Smith.

"Any price!" cried Leidesdorff, banging the table with his fist. "Next spring will see ships and wagon-trains reaching California, people pouring in! General Kearny with an army is on the way now from Santa Fe—settlers will follow by the thousand! By spring there'll be a famine of building materials here—"

"That isn't saying what you'd give per thousand for brick, inside the next three weeks," said Smith.

Leidesdorff roared out a fantastic figure, and Smith nodded.

"All right. Remember it," he said, "Might hold you to it."

"You?" Leidesdorff gave him a look. "Young man, are you joking?"

Smith grinned. "I was talking with a feller the other day said he could make bricks out of sea-water. Might be, Cap'n. Just remember what you'd pay."

A general laugh greeted his words, and the party broke up.

Sutter's launch arrived next afternoon, having made an un-usually quick trip, and the clerk in charge gave Smith the in-voices for the wagons and received a bill on Ward & Smith—hard cash was a rare thing, almost unknown, in Yerba Buena. The four wagons, all in pieces, were stacked on the beach above high-water mark, and Smith hastened to get in touch with Sullivan.

"Those wagons are yours, mind," he said. "When people get asking questions, as they will. You'll have to put one wagon together at a time, fetch horses, and drive away. Where will you keep them?"

"I can use one of the sheds at the old mission."

"Fine. How about the bricks?"

Sullivan grinned. "They are coming in fast, piles of them already. It will be a week more before we have them all. A good many cannot be reached in deeper water."

"Never mind; we'll have enough. It need be no secret that you're doing the job for me, or rather for Ward & Smith. As soon as you have one wagon running, start bringing them over. Pile 'em at the back of the store."

This village of exiles from the civilized world was a great place for gossip. The interest of everyone in everyone else's affairs was intense. Before another twenty-four hours it was known that the huge pile of stuff on the beach comprised a number of wagons; some said belonging to Ward & Smith, others that the wagons had already been sold to Sullivan.

Great was the merriment at thought of wagons in Yerba Buena, whose streets were thick sand-dust half the year, thicker quagmires of mud the other half. Occasionally an ox-cart, a *carreta* with thick slab wheels, came squeaking up into town with a load of adobe bricks—a frightfully slow and cumbersome method of transportation—and seldom could those slab wheels get through the thick sand or thicker mud.

WARD HEARD about it, came over to Brannan's house and had a long talk with his junior partner that evening. Smith laid everything before him frankly, including all he hoped to do; until now, he had kept it to himself. Frank Ward nodded thoughtfully.

"Abel, you're smart. I don't know about this village getting any bigger, though. It might develop into a town, years from now, in that case, and if Sullivan kept the teaming business in his own hands, we'd find it profitable to have an interest in it. As it stands, we're not out very much and have little to lose. Don't count too much on your hopes in regard to those adobe bricks down the bay shore, though."

"Why not?" demanded Smith. "Isn't the notion a good one?"

"Looks to be. But other men in Yerba Buena are smart, too— remember that! So far wagons have been unknown here. Now that they're actually here, I'll bet a dozen men are figuring right now how to put 'em to use. You'll see."

Sullivan lost no time in getting to work. Among the Mormon colonists who had arrived in July with Brannan's ship, many of whom had remained here, were a number of carpenters and wheelwrights. Sullivan had them hard at work Monday morning, and crowds of citizens gathered to watch the wagons being gradually assembled; by evening, one stood complete, to the general admiration.

Brannan, between his flour mills and printing press and a dozen other speculative affairs, was like a buzz-saw gone wild;

and Abel Smith threatened to be in like condition ere long. Monday night Sullivan sought him out in some excitement.

"Say, a feller offered me five hundred dollars today for two of them wagons!"

"Who?" Smith demanded.

"Kanaka Davis."

"Don't sell at any price. Don't sell or rent or anything else," said Smith firmly. Honest Sullivan was dismayed and even rebellious, but finally gave up protesting and went sadly away, half convinced that the young man from Nantucket had lost his senses.

Next morning Smith told his partner of the incident, jubilant that his own acuity was thus confirmed, but Frank Ward shook his head.

"I dunno, Abel. Davis is mighty 'cute; you have to get up early to beat him. Hello, here comes your greaser friend, with another in tow!"

Don Miguel was walking into the store, bringing his brother, a younger and dirtier and swarthier figure, whose serape was old and tattered. Frank Ward, in common with other foreigners, might be excused for talking of greasers and viewing them with contempt; but in sober fact their lands were measured by the square mile, their resources were great, and the older and more tattered a serape was, the more valuable it might be.

Smith shook hands, was introduced to Don Pedro de Rosa, the brother, and put his weird Spanish to work; it provoked much merriment, which was good for mutual harmony. Yes, Don Pedro had many thousands of adobe bricks which had been drying for from two to three months; very fine bricks, but hard to move all the way to Yerba Buena, since a *carreta* could not bring a large load and each brick was heavy.

How many? Oh, many thousand—vaguely, with a sweep of the hand. No more could be made now until spring came and hot sunlight to dry them, but tile could be burned in the kiln. Tile for roofs, tile for floors.

"I would like to buy all the bricks you have there," said Smith slowly, "and leave them until spring. Can you protect them from the rains?"

"Easily, señor."

"Then let tts talk about a price for the lot. In such a quantity, ten dollars is too much."

To Don Pedro, those adobes were only the product of a little laughing labor of many men, product of the earth and sunlight; if they sold for anything at all, so much the better for him. Men's labor was worth very little. He was going across up the bay to San Rafael with his brother Don Miguel, then return here in a few days. He would be glad to pick up some things in the store for his señora and the niños.

They settled on a price—as nearly as Smith could estimate, it ran to seven dollars per thousand, payment in trade, of course. The brothers shook hands and departed.

"Looks like a bang-up good buy, Abel," said Frank Ward upon hearing about it. This approbation was warming to Smith's soul.

One by one, the four wagons were assembled and driven away; then the bricks began to come in, several loads a day, the wagon coming across the sand hills out of nowhere, apparently. As the pile behind the store of Ward & Smith began to assume proportions, the village took excited note, and what promised at first to be a tremendous mystery, was of course soon run to earth.

Smith dropped in upon Captain Leidesdorff, who welcomed him with a bellow of delight and shoved a Manila cigar at him and fell to laughing.

"You and your bricks from seawater! I heard about it. What are you going to do with all that brick, young man?"

"Sell to you, since you undertook to buy them at your own price," Smith's blue eyes twinkled, then took warning. Leidesdorff's mirth was just a bit too hearty. "You wouldn't go back on a bargain, Captain?"

"Old Leidesdorff never goes back on a bargain, young man!" roared the other, and fell to laughing again.

"And that's not all," said Smith. "The minute the rains are over, wouldn't you like to have right here under your hand between ten and twenty thousand slabs of the finest adobe well mixed with straw and thoroughly seasoned? The entire available supply. There won't be any more for building purposes until they've hardened a couple of months—the middle of next summer, say. At twenty-one dollars per thousand, set down here in Yerba Buena. Think of that, Captain. Think what it'll mean."

Smith, having finished, sat back, lit his cigar, and relaxed happily. Leidesdorff drummed on the desk with his fingers and regarded him for a moment, no longer laughing.

"Adobes from the Rosa place, eh? You ask a high price."

"Delivered here."

"Oh!" Leidesdorff frowned. "I smell something and I don't like it, my friend—for your sake. From the day you came ashore and struck me for a job, I have liked you. Oh, maybe we quarrel now and then; I quarrel with everybody. But you are straight, and I say you are a friend."

"What do you mean?" asked Smith uneasily. "Do you mean the price is too high?"

"Price be damned! No!" returned the captain. "Look! Somewhere is something wrong. Kanaka Davis offers to sell me those bricks; they belong to him. They came from that old schooner belonging to Grimes & Davis that was wrecked on the outside coast a while back. What is more, Davis offers to sell me ten thousand adobes from the Rosa place whenever I want them."

Smith gulped. "When was this?"

"Before lunch. This morning."

"But he can't do it! I agreed with him about those bricks—Don Pedro de Rosa sold me all the adobes he had ready!"

"I am sorry." Leidesdorff spread his big hands helplessly. "I tell you this because I am a friend. There is something wrong."

SMITH DEPARTED stunned, absolutely stunned. Then anger took hold of him; by the time he was back at the store, he was breathing fire and fury. He poured his troubles into the ears of Frank Ward; never in his life had he been in such a rage.

"Wait a minute," said Ward. "You had an agreement with Davis. Let's see it."

"See it? We just agreed."

"And I thought you were a Yankee!"

"A bargain's a bargain in this town," stormed Smith. "A hand-shake's enough; nobody requires an agreement in writing."

"True. All the safer to have it, Abel."

"I'll have him up before the alcalde!" raged Smith. "And that rascal Don Pedro, too—I'll go after both of them if it costs me my last cent—"

"Hold on. When a man's angry he has no wits left. Slow down. Do nothing, say nothing, until an hour from now; just think, and try to think calmly," said Ward. "Then we'll see what's to be done. At worst, it won't break us."

"No man's going to do that to me and get away with it!" cried Smith furiously.

None the less, he was swift to calm down, because the wisdom of his partner's advice was obvious. An hour passed; he was clear-headed once more, but in the depths. The money loss would not be great, true. But his planning would go to the advantage of another, and he would be the laughing-stock of Yerba Buena; and nothing so rankles in the soul as the sense of injustice and trickery.

He was out in back, smoking his pipe and looking at the handsome pile of bricks, when Ward came out.

"I think your greaser friend is here—looks like him."

"Oh! Don Pedro? Good!" Smith knocked out his pipe and they went inside. Up front Don Pedro in his frayed serape was loafing about; but Frank Ward stopped suddenly.

"Look! Now what? That's Davis, and Lieutenant Bartlett with him—and Sullivan!"

The three were just entering—brawny Kanaka Davis, Bartlett of the *Portsmouth,* who since the raising of the Stars and Stripes over Yerba Buena had been acting alcalde, or magistrate and mayor; and with them, Sullivan, looking angry. Bartlett, brisk and authoritative, nodded amiably to the partners.

"Hello, boys. Want to have a word with you. Can we close the store for privacy?"

"Sure," replied Ward. "I'll do it."

"Don't clear out Don Pedro!" yelped Smith. "Let him stay! I don't want to miss him."

HE EXCHANGED one grim look with Kanaka Davis, and took the visitors to the office in the rear. Frank Ward joined them, with the door closed.

"All right, gentlemen. Now what's it all about?"

"Nothing official—but it might be," said Bartlett. "In brief, Mr. Davis complains to me that Mr. Sullivan, here, is taking bricks that belong to him and piling them back of this store. Sullivan says he is working for Ward & Smith, so we came to see you about it."

"Is this a trial?" Frank Ward demanded. Bartlett smiled.

"No. This alcalde is trying to save trouble. This is a friendly hearing. Davis, let's have your case."

"The bricks are from a wrecked ship belonging to my firm," said Davis. "Each brick is stamped with a maker's mark. I can prove it easily enough."

"And you agreed with me," spoke up Smith, keeping his temper down, "that if I recovered them and gave you twenty per cent of them, you'd be satisfied to let me keep the rest. You don't deny it, do you?"

Davis eyed him. Denial would mean calling someone a liar— and Abel Smith had not worked his passage to California aboard a whaler without developing muscle. His bright blue eyes were a sure indication of what would happen, once the word passed.

"No," said Davis. "But that was for a few bricks only, as much as a man could carry, or thereabouts. Not the whole shipload!"

"You're a liar and you know it!" barked Smith.

Bartlett intervened. "That's enough of that, gentlemen. Silence! Apologize, Smith."

"Be damned if I will!" said Smith hotly.

"I'm sure nobody thinks Mr. Davis is a liar," cut in Frank Ward, in his pleasant way. "Forgive my junior partner's anger, Mr. Davis; he's a bit unreasonable, perhaps."

"Is there any written agreement about those bricks?" Bartlett demanded. "No? Then, I take it the issue lies between Mr. Davis and Ward & Smith?"

"That's it, Lieutenant," said Frank Ward. Smith was having a low word aside with Sullivan, who now spoke up.

"Then am I haulin' these brick for Davis?"

"You sure are," snapped Davis angrily.

"All right," said Sullivan. "You got no pay agreed on. It'll cost you one hundred dollars a load, mister—all the way over them sandhills, plus recovering the bricks out of the water."

"No, it will not," spoke up Bartlett. "No such extortion goes on in Yerba Buena, Sullivan. Now, you gentlemen keep quiet. Let me point up this matter."

Smith's heart fell; Bartlett was dead against him.

"Smith, you've got nothing to prove your word, but I don't doubt it," Bartlett proclaimed. "Same for you, Davis. Let's say there's been a mistake and let it go at that. Now, those bricks were lying in a wreck, I understand?"

"In and out," said Davis. "They've been there a couple years."

"Abandoned, eh? I suppose you couldn't retrieve them?"

"Wasn't worth while without a boat to haul 'em in." Davis began to be surly.

"Oh!" Lieutenant Bartlett bit at a cigar. "Now they're recovered. That's what is called salvage, Mr. Davis; Mr. Smith has salvaged them, and is therefore entitled legally to eighty per centum of their value-—maybe more. I haven't looked up the law."

HE PAUSED. Smith plucked up hope once more. Davis, beneath his scowl, showed a faint indication of a twinkle; after all, he had no more than tried to get ahead of a smart Yankee.

"Now, if you want this alcalde to sit in a regular court," went on Bartlett, "he'll do it. There'll be fees to pay and also the devil to pay. You all know how those Mormons got after Sam Brannan and held the first jury trial in California, and Sam and the alcalde were the only ones who got anything out of it. I wouldn't advise you gentlemen to repeat the experiment.

"Therefore and whereas and so forth," he added with a chuckle, "I advise you, Smith, to keep eighty per centum of the brick, and you, Davis, to take twenty per centum and be damned glad you got 'em; and both parties to shake hands in presence of the court. Thereafter everybody adjourning to John Henry Brown's saloon for a drink. And so endeth the first unofficial court decision in the district of Yerba Buena, so help you God!"

Abel Smith and Davis exchanged a look. Resentment clashed with surly dislike.

"I never had much use for a brash Yankee," said Kanaka Davis, and put out his hand. "But you might be worse, Smith. Shake hands and forget it?"

"Come to think of it, we didn't shake hands on the other deal," said Smith, and took the proffered fist. "Let's do it now, and forget it."

He found the dour gaze of Davis suddenly friendly. Between them, oddly enough, sprang a swift amity, a clearance, even a twinkling smile, where a moment ago had been enmity. Just mutual acquaintance taking hold, perhaps.

"Come on, everybody, let's go!" exclaimed Davis. "The drinks are on me."

They all started for the doors. Then Smith sighted the lurking, loitering figure of Don Pedro, to whom all this jabbering of English had been a mystery. He spoke up.

"You folks go along. I'll be right over. Got to see Don Pedro a minute."

The others trooped out, laughing and talking loudly. Smith approached the Californian and eyed him, trying to summon up some angry Spanish. The man had basely tricked him; he meant to be harsh about it, too.

"Ha, señor!" he began. "You agreed to sell me all those adobes of yours at seven dollars a thousand."

"*Si, señor,*" said the other in his gentle smiling way. "That is correct."

"But Señor Davis is also selling some of your adobes here! How can that be? Are you breaking your agreement with me?"

Don Pedro looked both startled and shocked.

"*Pero, señor!* Does a *caballero,* a *viejo Cristiano,* a gentleman, break his word? Assuredly not!"

"Then how can Señor Davis be selling adobes from your place?"

White teeth flashed in a quick smile.

"It is like this. There are two big sheds that my father built long ago. In the walls are about ten thousand bricks of adobe. I will have them broken out and sold to the Señor Davis. They are old, weathered down, maybe broken." Don Pedro shrugged. "He does not care. It is all the same to him. You wanted only the fine new ones."

"Oh!" said Abel Smith. "Oh!"

As the explanation rushed over his mind, he was in turn shocked by his own suspicious thoughts of treachery. So simple!

Then he brightened. Wait till Leidesdorff heard about these old worthless slabs of adobe! Kanaka Davis would have a hard time unloading them on anyone in Yerba Buena! So. much the better for Ward & Smith—decidedly better. The thing was going through all right, just as he visioned it. His suspicions were groundless. He still had a monopoly on all the adobes to be had until next summer, and wagons to haul them.

"Come along, Don Pedro!" he exclaimed abruptly.

"Where, señor," queried the other. Smith clapped him on the back.

"Join us in a drink, *caballero*—I seldom drink, but today is a fine day, a great day; I have learned something. We'll all have a drink, to business as done by *caballeros* and gentlemen—eh?"

"*Seguro, si!*" said Don Pedro happily. "Sure!"

IV

OIL, IRON AND RAGS

*"You May Know That the Diamond in
Your Shirt Front Is Paste, but as Long as
No One Else Does, It Don't Matter"*

S INCE IT was Sunday, and Frank Ward was away shooting goats and geese on the islands in the bay, the store was
not open. Abel Smith, as junior partner, had the place all to
himself and was making various improvements, with hammer
and paint brush, when a furious assault on the front door
aroused him. He opened, and in stalked Sam Brannan.

"Hey! It's noon! Aren't you coming home to dinner? Why
didn't you come to church?" demanded Brannan, all in one
breath.

Smith stared at him. "Church! What church?"

Brannan grinned, flecked dust from his dandified attire, and
adjusted the imitation diamond in his shirt-front.

"My church. Ain't I a presiding elder in the Latter Day
Saints?"

"Thought they'd kicked you out."

"Now, now, we're in California, ain't we? What Brigham
Young does over at Salt Lake doesn't hold in Yerba Buena. We
had a fine sermon; I delivered it."

"Where? At John Henry Brown's saloon?" demanded Smith,
his bony features all agrin.

"No. On the plaza. Portsmouth Square, as it is now, in honor
of our noble vessel yonder which raised the Stars and Stripes
over the village in July. And, my friend, fully two-thirds of our
one hundred and sixty inhabitants attended the service. Why
didn't you?"

"Too hungry," said Smith. "Mrs. Brannan, my landlady, is sick and I didn't get any breakfast."

"Well, she'd better have dinner ready or Mr. Brannan will know the reason why!" said the ebullient Sam, fingering his black goatee. He seated himself on a counter and bit at a cigar. "Abel, we're making money. I'm tickled you came in with me on the flour-mill deal. I got an order this morning for a thousand pounds of flour from the frigate *Congress,* now in harbor. Another from the whaler *Jemima* for three hundred pounds. The *Congress* pays in money, the whaler in otter skins and sperm oil. You can take over the otter skins and ship 'em out and make money for the store. Dammit, you're making money two ways!"

Mr. Smith's bright blue eyes sparkled. He liked Yerba Buena. Since coming to California he had done well by himself, being a hard worker. He liked Sam Brannan, who was a soldier of fortune like everyone else here, only more so; in fact, he liked everybody.

"And," pursued Brannan, "Cap'n Lowry of the whaler wants to meet you. He's a Nantucket man himself, says he knows you. He's on his way home with a full ship, the lucky old gander! Says he's the last one of the season—we'll have outward bound vessels in port after this for a while."

"Lowry, sure! I remember him," said Smith. "What's that about outward bound ships? There's no whaling season. They come and go any time."

"Well, that's the gist of what he said, anyhow," Brannan rejoined. "There won't be any more whalers here, except empty ships bound for the Islands, for months. He said so. And he's coming ashore tomorrow to see you and order a bill of goods from the store. Let's go on home and see about dinner."

HE LOCKED up and they started for Brannan's house on Clay Street. There were all of fifty houses in Yerba Buena, though more were building fast. With immigrants coming in by wagon trains from across the plains, and more coming down

WARD & ~~SMITH~~

HUMISTON-

from Oregon to find a rainless paradise, Yerba Buena was getting her share of new settlers and was moving at a fast tempo.

They passed Leidesdorff's occupied but still unfinished store and home. His old adobe structure had been turned over to John Henry Brown, who was trying to get it fitted up as a hotel while hanging on to his saloon business; and Leidesdorff was already at work on a still larger structure. Everything was fast-moving.

"Hi! Abel Smith!" This was Leidesdorff, stentorian of voice, brawny and untidy and magnificent of person, the chief figure in town. "Hold on! I want a word with you!"

"But not with me," said Sam Brannan. "I'll run along, Abel, and see about dinner."

He stalked away. Leidesdorff rumbled up and buttonholed Smith, casting a dark look after Brannan. He did not fancy that grandiloquent, hypnotic young man of twenty-six. Leidesdorff

was thirty-four, settled in his ways, an ex-skipper from the
Danish West Indies, and the brawling youth surging around
him in Yerba Buena was disquieting. He liked Abel Smith,
though. Most people did like the young fellow from Nantucket with the bony features and the sparkling blue eyes.

"Now look," said Leidesdorff. "You got any sperm oil in
stock?"

"A little. Got some more coming ashore from that whaler
just arrived," said Smith.

"Send me over what you can spare in the morning, will you?
I put a couple barrels aboard the *Congress* this week and it nigh
cleaned me out."

"Glad to do it, Cap'n. Why don't you stock up from the
whaler yonder?"

"That damned Yankee skipper wants too much money. Whale
oil! Arrgh!" Leidesdorff roared his contempt. "Good for nothing
but lamps. Every whaler's running over with it; just like dirt.
No money in handling the stuff."

"Hm! Lot of lamps in California, though," observed Abel
Smith thoughtfully.

Leidesdorff pressed a Manila cigar on him; something else
was coming.

"You know what you spoke to me about—changing the name
of Yerba Buena?" said the captain in a confidential bellow. "You
haven't broached it to anyone else?"

"Not a soul, Cap'n."

"Well, don't. I've talked to O'Farrell about it. He's to be
trusted; he worked for John Sutter when he first got here, and
Sutter trusted him fully. It's going to be a hard thing to manage,
but we'll do it. So if Jasper mentions it to you, you'll know I
told him."

Smith nodded. It was the early fall of '46. The hamlet on this
little cove of Yerba Buena, in San Francisco Bay, was now under
the United States flag, and Leidesdorff had the firm conviction
that it was going to be a real city some day. Leidesdorff had a

finger in everything and a hundred irons in the fire, and his roaring energy would sooner or later heat them all red-hot, if the prophesied boom ever came.

"Sutter's launch came in last night," said Leidesdorff. "His clerk, Bidwell, came with it, and if you see him in any of the saloons, tell him I want him, will you?"

"Sure," agreed Smith cheerfully. "I don't use the saloons much, but I may run into him."

"If John Sutter thinks he can stick me with a lot of emigrants' truck sent down from Oregon, he's mistaken," grumbled the captain. Smith pricked up his ears.

"Emigrants' truck?" he repeated.

"Yes. Wagonloads of old clothes and stuff collected up there by a smart trader and worked off on Sutter. Trash, absolute trash! Well, young fellow, if your partner brings back a good bag from the islands yonder, tell him I'd like to have a tender young kid and a couple of geese. See you later."

Smith went his way to the Brannan house on Clay Street, which was a busy place seven days a week. Brannan had brought two flour-mills around the Horn with his Mormon ship; and while his Mormon enterprise and alliances had miscarried, the fact that he was able to turn out real American flour had not. It was being turned out enormously, and Smith was doing very nicely, thank you, between his partnership in Ward's store and Sam's flour mills.

Dinner was ready, and Brannan of the hypnotic eyes and nimble brain talked a blue streak. He could, on occasion keep very silent—a significant hint to anyone who knew men. Mrs. Brannan, an able and blooming young woman, adored Sam and liked to hear him orate; and Abel Smith, who always got ideas when other folks talked, listened happily and did justice to the meal.

Brannan had picked up all sorts of news. War news—the war with Mexico was going on, and southern California was rife with alarums and excursions, in which Yerba Buena took small interest. An army was coming overland to help occupy the country, said Sam. A brig was coming down from the Oregon coast with some fine furs for Mr. Astor. Captain Lowry's whaler still had a lot of iron ballast aboard he had brought out to sell at the islands—

"Iron ballast?" put in Smith. "That's in demand here. Sutter has a forge at his fort and Leidesdorff ships him iron."

"This is the wrong kind," said Brannan, laughing. "This is old plows and such stuff collected in New England—useless truck he had meant to work off on the Honolulu missionaries, but they were too smart for him and wouldn't have it. I told him California people used plows that were just forked sticks, and that disgusted him."

"It's true enough," said Smith. "But a lot of Americans who know about plows are coming into this country. More wagon trains will be along before winter."

"Well, he's got enough rusty plowshares to sink his ship!" said Brannan, chuckling. "Last I saw of him, he was going to drown his sorrows at Brown's saloon."

Local news, too, filled his plack. Leese's warehouse, at Sonoma, had burned with everything in it; Leese was the big merchant up there, had married Vallejo's sister-in-law and was rich enough to stand the loss. A new saw mill, rumor said, was soon to be set up; this would be bad news for Leidesdorff, who had a grip on all the lumber business in town. Lieutenant Bartlett of the *Portsmouth,* acting alcalde or chief magistrate and mayor of Yerba Buena, had had a dispute with Commodore Stockton, who wanted him to return to duty aboard ship… and so forth, endlessly.

Abel Smith hurried through the meal; his head was buzzing with several ideas that clamored for attention and prompt action, but not over-prompt. His partner was not at hand to consult, and had learned the truth of the old adage that two heads were better than one. Moreover, Frank Ward was twenty-four, his senior by two years, and had drilled him in the wisdom of making haste slowly where business was concerned. He tried, honestly enough, to make no haste, but circumstances were against him today.

He went around to the blacksmith shop of Finch and Thompson. It was closed; the saloon adjoining, also owned by Finch & Thompson, was open, and Finch was in the back room trying to cut his hair with a pair of rusty shears. Smith lent him a hand and got his mane trimmed, and posed the questions that were demanding answer. Finch reflected over his pipestem and finally nodded.

"If a plowshare ain't too far gone with rust, I reckon it can be brought up," he stated. "If it ain't wore down too much, that is. All depends. It can be a lot wore down and still be good for work. That is, if a feller ain't too particular."

"Fine!" said Smith. "See you later about the job."

He went on to John Henry Brown's saloon. Here, sitting over a hot toddy in the back corner was Captain Dan Lowry, frosty-eyed as ever. He wore grizzled galleghers like a hanging fringe from ear to ear, and had a habit of waving them gently with his finger-tips as he ruminated. His lips were thin and tight, but when Abel Smith hove into sight he thawed out his shell of whaling-master's dignity, shook hands heartily, and insisted that Abel join him in a tot of rum.

"Heard you was here," he said. "Ain't seen you goin' on three years—and how you've growed! So you're in business for yourself out here, are you?"

"We've got a little store," said Smith modestly. "Doing all right. Now, tell me about the Hawkins folks, Cap'n Dan…"

THEY TALKED Nantucket for a bit. Lowry observed that he might drop into the store on the morrow, and Smith suggested that he could do it now.

"I'm surprised, right surprised at you, Abel Smith," said the skipper severely. "I don't do business of a Sabbath. No Godfearing man would. And you with your upbringing ought to know better."

"Wouldn't you put the boats out for a whale if you saw a spout on Sunday?"

"That's different. That's doing the Lord's work, if so be as He intended us to make a kill on that day."

"All right, then; no business till tomorrow, Cap'n Dan," assented Smith. "I don't reckon you got much demand for sperm oil around here, have you?"

"Oh, a bar'l here and a bar'l there," said the captain, and glanced up as a man stopped beside them. It was Howard, of Mellus & Howard, a genial, open-hearted young fellow whom Smith rather liked.

"What!" he exclaimed. "Are our competitors talking about buying sperm oil?"

"No much, Bill," said Smith, and introduced the captain. "Leidesdorff was asking me to send him over some. If you have any to spare for him, I'll be glad of it."

Howard shook his head. "A barrel of that stuff goes a long way," he said. "We've got enough to last us a while, but none to spare. Well, glad to have met you, Cap'n."

He went his way. Smith, filling his pipe, relaxed.

"I know where there'd be a demand for about fifty barrels of that stuff," he observed casually. "But the price would have to be right. Of course, some whaler captain who had rather sell cheap here than carry the oil back to Nantucket, might be satisfied to make a quick turnover. However, we'll talk about that later. Do you know, Cap'n Dan, something that would make the proper ballast for a schooner?"

Captain Lowry's aimless eye came to life.

"Ballast? What d'ye mean, Abel?"

"Well, Leidesdorff has a schooner that brings lumber down from the mill at Bodega, up the coast," Smith explained. "He was talking to me this morning about it. Seems like he has a lot of trouble, or his skipper has, getting the proper ballast for the schooner."

"Huh!" sniffed Captain Dan. "Fine cockeyed kind of a sailor

he must be! If it's well stowed against shifting, ain't nothing better than iron—any old iron. Take old plowshares f'rinstance."

"Folks don't use 'em out here," Smith rejoined. "They use a forked tree limb, shaped for the work. That's all the soil in California needs. If I knew where to pick up some iron like that, I might make a couple dollars on the deal."

"I got a mess of it aboard," said the captain. "If I fill my No. 2 hold on the v'yage home, I'd have to dump it overboard. Might talk about it tomorrow, Abel."

"So we might," agreed Smith brightly. "Remind me of it, in case I forget, will you?

They talked for some time longer. Smith had worked his passage out to California aboard a whaler, they had many things and friends in common, and Captain Lowry accepted an invitation to supper very gladly; he had given most of his crew liberty for the day and was remaining to pick them all up before nightfall.

Upon leaving Captain Lowry, Smith went home, informed Mrs. Brannan that he would have a guest for supper, and then stepped forth anew. He had some difficulty in locating John Bidwell; Sutter's chief clerk and assistant was soon quitting his post to head for Monterey and more congenial work at that capital of the country, and had a host of friends in Yerba Buena.

Smith finally ran him to earth where he had begun his own afternoon, in Finch's saloon, engaged in conversation with Finch's partner, the brawny Thompson, who had been a blacksmith in the Cherokee Nation. Bidwell was getting some information about smelting iron for the benefit of Sutter's forge workmen. Abel Smith joined them, and when Thompson went off to tend bar, he engaged Bidwell in talk.

"What's this Leidesdorff tells me about you trying to put off some old clothes on him?" he demanded, laughingly. Bidwell snorted.

"Leidesdorff is pig-headed when he gets a notion," he said. "This isn't old clothes as he is persuaded it is. It's a lot of odds

and ends picked up in Oregon and sent down here on consignment. You know, the tremendous rush of immigration from the
East has left a lot of broken hearts up there—people who
couldn't make good, and cleared out, after bringing no end of
useless stuff from the East. Odds and ends of clothing, house-
hold goods, books, every damned thing you can imagine and
can't use. Leidesdorff, blast him, has spread the word that we're
trying to sell old clothes, and everybody's laughing at me."

"I'm not," said Smith. "How much of the stuff is there?"

"It'd make a full cargo for the fifty-ton launch."

"I wouldn't take it on consignment; we'd have to make a deal
outright."

"I could do that, too," said Bidwell.

"And Ward & Smith would have to make a dollar somewhere
along the line, mind that!"

"All right, Yankee, all right," said the other, laughing. "The
stuff is in packing cases, some in burlap or leather bags. We
have no invoice; everything from pots and pans to bustles and
hoop-skirts. You can have the lot for six hundred dollars."

Smith was aghast. "For old clothes? Come, come, Bidwell!
Half that stuff will have to be given away to get rid of it. I'll
give you a hundred flat."

After twenty minutes they compromised on three hundred,
delivery, to be made by the next trip of Sutter's big launch. It
was a deal, for better or for worse.

Captain Lowry, in his best blue broadcloth and brass buttons,
was an impressive dinner guest that evening. He even impressed
Sam Brannan, who had wandered all over the country and seen
everything. Dinner over, they sat and talked on until the lamps
were lit.

"What you got in that lamp, sperm oil?" the skipper asked.
"Thought so. That reminds me, Abel. How many bar'ls of sperm
do you want?"

"Thought you wouldn't do business today?" said Smith.

"Sabbath ends at sunset," said Captain Dan, fanning his

fringe of whiskers. "I can make you a good proposition on, say, forty bar'l. And if you got a mind to them plowshares, we might talk it over."

Smith was willing to discuss the matter. Now forty barrels of sperm-head oil totted up to a bit of money. The argument was long; Lowry extolled the ability of his coopers and the excellence of his casks. Smith hung off, backed and filled, finally put off giving any definite response until the morrow, and left it that way.

When the guest had departed, Sam Brannan inspected his friend thoughtfully.

"You young devil, you!"

"Meaning what?" asked Smith, his eyes dancing.

"You know I've got that ranch on the Stanislaus River—had a chance to pick it up cheap, and now I'm going to sell it again. You know why?"

"You've decided to stay in Yerba Buena, sure."

"No, I've tried high and low to get a plowshare in this cursed country, and can't. They plow with a crooked stick. Sutter says he can make some in his forge—and you ought to know what could be done here with a real plow. Even an old one is good."

"Or a hundred. Or two hundred," said Abel Smith. "Lowry has about four hundred, he says, old and rusty. I figure half of 'em may be good, when they're worked over."

"Be damned if I'm not going into the store business myself!" said Brannan.

FRANK WARD showed up that evening, tired and triumphant, with a boatload of birds and kids to hand out among his friends. Told of Leidesdorff's request, he promptly sent a kid and several birds over to the captain, who planned one of his gargantuan feasts for Commodore Stockton.

Next day Lowry came into the store and gave a big order for his slopchest and his galley. Smith handled him, and before the interview was done, had made highly satisfactory arrangements including forty barrels of oil and a mass of old iron guaranteed to contain at least four hundred plowshares. Since Frank Ward knew nothing of the deal, Smith went about his own business and let it rest. On the following day, however, the iron and oil began to come ashore, and the heavens opened.

"What's this about oil?" said Frank Ward, pinning the junior partner into a corner. "And rusty old iron?"

Smith explained. Ward shook his head.

"I don't like it. Blast it, you've gone and committed us again, without consulting me! You know a barrel of oil will last us a month. These ideas of your will ruin us!"

"You've liked 'em so far," protested Smith. "It was my notion to buy those two launches and start 'em running clear around the whole bay, picking up hides and tallow at different spots—"

"So far, everything's all right," said Ward. "But I'm not sure about this deal with Lowry. He bought a big order, and all we get is oil and old iron."

"And about fifty prime sea-otter skins to boot," said Smith. This helped the thing blow over, for the moment; otter skins made profitable trade.

A couple of days later O'Farrell dropped in before taking a trip up to Sonoma, where he had a small ranch, and consulted with Smith.

"Leidesdorff tells me, my nimble-witted Yankee, of your grand idea to knock the spots off the new town that's being planned up the bay," said he, a twinkle in his jaunty eye. "Larkin and Vallejo and that crowd, with their new town of Francesca, planning *to* make it the city of the future—oh, glory be!"

"Hush!" exclaimed Smith, glancing around. "Don't talk so loud, Jasper—"

"All right, all right, me lad," said the Irishman. "Anyhow, Leidesdorff is working like hell in various quarters. All of a sudden the cat will be out of the bag; this Yerba Buena of ours will get itself organized, and we'll turn it into San Francisco—

yes, it's a great idea! Well, what about my buying some hides
and tallow up north for your account?"

"No. But listen! There are loads of American settlers around
there, all up the Nappa valley. Tell 'em we're getting in some
real American plows, Jasper—second hand, but good. Don't
know the price yet."

O'Farrell. grinned. "You don't mean that rust-heap outside?"

"They'll be put into first-class condition. Guaranteed."

"All right, me lad! Your blood be upon your own head. *Adios!*"

THE DAYS passed. The full amount of oil came ashore,
and was stacked behind the store; there was no room in the
warehouse, for merchandise was coming in from the east, one
vessel and another arriving. The full amount of old iron came
in, and Captain Dan Lowry put out to sea.

Now, Frank Ward and Abel Smith were friends and partners,
and were making money, and Ward really held his Yankee
partner in considerable regard. But he was a New Yorker, something of a gay blade yet serious at bottom, and if there was one
thing on earth he could by no means stomach, it was ridicule.

Finch & Thompson, meantime, were working on the heap
of old iron, and promised very good results in bringing the
plowshares out into some sort of usable condition. This made
Abel Smith happy. He was toiling far too hard to get around
town very much or to mingle with competitors—competition
in Yerba Buena being a jovial, merciless, hard-bitten thing.

He did notice that Ward was getting a cranky humor, and
accordingly worked the harder to please his partner. It had scant
effect. Ward became crankier every day, apt to fly off the handle
at any provocation; he was, as a matter of fact, beginning to
catch bursts of raillery from every angle. Smith was vaguely
aware of the gathering storm, but not of its cause. He was really
working. Others could take time off to loaf around the embarcadero or the bars and talk with folks, but he was always pushing
an idea or doing something to the store—hunting, fishing,
recreation, were impossible, at the moment.

They would come in good time.

Two schooners from the Islands came into the bay, bringing a bit of merchandise; after the other recent arrivals from the east, this stocked all the shelves in town. The new settlers flocked into town and out again. Rancheros and their wives and vaqueros trooped in to buy. Business was rising to a peak when, one afternoon, Sutter's big launch arrived from the Sacramento and got some of her cargo up to Ward & Smith, and her crew, circulating around, did some talking.

Frank Ward had been out with John Henry Brown, helping to equip what was to be the barman's new hotel, and came in just at closing time. He was white to the lips.

"Come on, shut up the place," he said curtly. "Want to see you alone."

The extra clerk was sent off. The doors were closed. The two partners, in the office, faced one another and Smith knew that it was worse than a storm.

"What's wrong, Frank?" he asked anxiously.

Ward, with difficulty, kept himself in hand.

"I'll stand no more of it," he said. "It's the last straw. For days now, they've been making jokes about using oil on that heap of old iron; the whole town has been jeering at us. I took it all and said nothing. I was trying to play the game with you and back you up—but this—this—it's too much."

"This what?" demanded Abel Smith.

"This deal with Sutter. Is it true, what they say—that you let Bidwell sting you? That this stuff they've been sending up from his launch is a lot of old clothes? Did you buy it off him?"

"Yes," said Smith. "But it's not old clothes, Frank—and listen to me, will you?"

"Talk," Ward snapped out.

"About that oil, now. There just isn't any; there won't be any whalers in for months. Cap'n Lowry told me so. Leese's warehouse at Sonoma burned; took all his oil with it. Nobody has

any. Nobody will have any. We've got all there is, Frank, and
got it cheap too!"

"Are you done?" asked Ward, as his partner paused. His voice
was bitter hard, his face was set and cold, his eyes were pools
of black ice.

"No. Be reasonable, now! That iron—I told you there were
a lot of plowshares in the pile. That's so. Hundreds. Just what
people here are wanting like blazes, Frank. These are being
worked over by Finch & Thompson. They'll sell like hot cakes.
Every rancher up the Sacramento, up the Nappa, will want
'em—and none are to be had at any price! Sutter forges a plow
or two occasionally, poor stuff, too. What aren't plowshares here,
I'll sell him as old iron for his forges. We aren't going to lose a
dollar on it, Frank!"

"We've already lost more than money can buy back," said
Ward coldly. "Forty barrels of whale oil—a small mountain of
rusty old iron—and now this, this! Old clothes! Pots and pans!
Gimcracks, bustles, hoop-skirts—good God! You've made Ward
& Smith the laughing stock of the whole town!"

"Let 'em laugh!" said Abel Smith stoutly. "It's the last laugh
that counts!"

"Spoken like a Yankee, sure enough," Ward barked out cuttingly. "The proclamation post over on the plaza—the square,
I mean—has a big 'Old Clo' sign on it, over our names. The
town's making us the butt of ridicule this minute. You don't see
people laughing and poking jokes at Leidesdorff or Henry
Mellus or Grimes & Davis—no, sir! A merchant must have his
dignity; a business is respected only while it stands for something in the community."

"Frank, I'm sorry," Smith said earnestly. "But you're wrong
about the old clothes. That's a lot of odds and ends, I know—"

He was cut short by a blaze of profanity. Frank Ward was in
no mood to listen to reason; he had been too long listening to
pitiless ridicule, and it smarted to the quick. Abel Smith sat
twisting his fingers, incredulous, heartsick at the realization

that his partner was actually in a whole-hearted fury that would brook no explanations, a white-lipped rage of utter abandon.

"You've had plenty of warnings to discuss your damned Yankee notions with me before committing the firm," cracked Ward in conclusion. "Now we're through, Abel. You've played me this dastardly trick for the last time ever! We'll get the books gone over and straighten out your quarter interest, and when that's done your name comes off the sign and you can do what you please."

"Frank! You don't mean that—you can't mean it!" burst out Smith, his bony features contorted with dismay, his eyes stricken and grief-filled. "Why, Frank, we're friends!"

"Friends, but no longer partners," said Ward with finality. "My mind's made up; we're through. Go on out into the town and get laughed at, jeered at from every side, like I've been this afternoon! Why, I can hardly sit in this chair without wanting to writhe and scream like a hysterical woman—that's how it feels!"

HE SPRANG to his feet. "And get your blasted oil and junk iron off this property, and do it tomorrow! Take your—your rags and bones with the rest, understand? You and your fine talk about people wanting to buy such trash—oil and old iron and used clothes! Our shelves are filled; every store in town is crammed to bursting with merchandise, and you think people are coming in to buy from a firm that's the joke of Yerba Buena? To buy old trash that's dredged up from the gutters? We're through, Abel, we're through! I want the business of gentlemen like Stockton and Captain Montgomery and Don Mariano Vallejo, not the trade of vaqueros and common seamen before the mast, buying castoff shoes and pants! Get all of your stuff off this property before tomorrow night or I'll put it in the street. Good night."

He strode out of the store in a white heat of anger, disregarding Smith's appealing voice, and the door slammed.

Abel Smith sat for a long while with drooping head and eyes

of misery, staring at nothing, while the shadows gathered outside, and from the bay drifted the double strokes of ship's bells striking the hour. He saw nothing, heard nothing, except the face and voice of Frank Ward in bitter accusation.

Gone, swept away, were all his high hopes and glorious prospects—struck down at one blow. For weeks he had given his whole self, his entire energy, to this firm and its growth. He had been proud beyond words of Ward & Smith; now it was gone in scorn and contempt that enveloped him like an icy blast. Within himself was the conviction that all he had done was well justified and well done; yet, at the same time, he could bitterly see that Frank Ward was also justified. From Ward's angle, those searing accusations had full excuse.

Outside, a man came to the door, tried it, opened it, and stepped in. He came to the office in the rear and saw the silent, drooped figure there. It was Sam Brannan.

"Good God, Abel! What's the matter?" exclaimed Brannan. Smith looked up at him, let his head fall again, said nothing. Brannan came inside the railing and hit him on the shoulder. "Wake up! What's gone wrong?"

Smith roused himself, and in the dead tones of utter despair, told what had taken place and why. Brannan cursed with all the fluency of a veteran journeyman printer, but when he fell to cursing Frank Ward, Smith stopped him.

"No, Sam, no—don't say that! Frank's all right. What he did—I guess—was the right thing; looked so to him, anyhow. He never could stand being joked."

Brannan sank down, put his arm about the disconsolate shoulders, and spoke his heart. Gone was the cynical, dandified adventurer, the flambuoyant poseur; here in the gloom was Sam Brannan the man, pitying, helping, encouraging with all the hypnotic eloquence and bright radiance of spirit he could command.

"Now forget everything and come along to supper, and let tomorrow bury its own dead," he concluded. "I'll lend you a hand in the morning and we'll use the flour-mill workmen. We can stack the barrels and iron back of my house, and get the stuff from Sutter's launch brought up there. Stay away from Ward for a few days. The flour is selling like mad—I got an order from Leese at Sonoma, today, for a thousand pounds. We are making money. We'll be laughing at Frank Ward yet."

"Maybe, but it'll still hurt," said Smith, pulling himself together.

"Sure. Lots of things have hurt me, but I'm still going strong. That's what it means to be a man, to carry a hurt in your heart and a smile on your lips! I had a grand newspaper in New Orleans, and it went bust on me between two days…"

Sam Brannan talked of his failures, as they went home together; something he had never before done. Talked of them brilliantly, told how they still hurt, and laughed at them.

"Two things, Abel—never take yourself very seriously, and never take the other fellow too seriously; they'll pull you through anything. I can pull a long face and preach sermons and be a Mormon elder, and thumb my nose at Brigham Young if he kicks me out. I can start a newspaper, and if it fails, go on somewhere else and start one, like I mean to do here. Grin at yourself, and to hell with sobersides! The diamond in my shirt-front is paste and I know it, but others don't."

A peculiar philosophy but a cheering one. By the time they reached the house, Abel Smith was smiling once again, though with a quaver in the smile; and at the table he was almost his usual self. Two-and-twenty can recover swiftly from blows that at forty would be crushing, and at sixty, mortal.

Next day—well, it was pretty tough to stay out of the store that meant so much, and fall to work getting the oil and iron moved, and to see the little mountain of boxes and cases and bundles pile up at the side of the house. Smith began to realize more acutely just how Frank Ward had suffered, for jibes were poured on him from every hand, and half the town seemed to come past just in order to make jocular comment. This worried him not at all, but he could see what torment it must mean to Ward.

NOBODY KNEW the facts. Ward kept his mouth shut, and not a soul except Brannan knew of the dissolved partnership that was ahead. When the oil and iron was stowed behind Sam Brannan's house, and the cases and boxes neatly stacked beside it, facing the vacant lots, Brannan fetched horses, ordered Abel Smith into the saddle, and rode with him down the sandy trail toward Santa Clara.

They were gone for three days, visiting at ranchos where a visit involved festivity and a fandango, if not more extended hospitality. When, on the third evening, they jogged back to Yerba Buena, Smith felt as though he had been in another world.

"I can see it through without a quiver," he told Brannan, and smiled. "Tomorrow I'll walk into the store and settle up with Frank, and walk out like a man, thanks to you. I don't know why I was so broken up that evening—it just got me."

It was after dark when they got home, and Mrs. Brannan rustled up some cold grub. O'Farrell had been here twice looking for Smith, she said; so had Frank Ward, only this afternoon. And O'Farrell had taken one of those burlapped bundles from the big pile outside; she supposed it was all right, him being a friend.

"Oh, sure," said Smith carelessly. "Did Ward say what he wanted?"

"Said to tell you to come over to the store when you got back, that's all."

After supper, Brannan went out to circulate around, and Smith, saddlesore, went to bed and slept life a log. He slept late, too; he did not waken until somebody shook him and he sat up to see Brannan and O'Farrell, both of them laughing. A buzz of voices reached him.

"What's going on?" he demanded, yawning. "Who's that talking?"

"There's a crowd outside, waiting for you," said Brannan. "Hurry up! Get into your duds and grab a bite to eat—tell him, Jasper, while I go amuse the crowd."

He vanished. O'Farrell, all agrin, made report.

"I hate to say it, Abel, but you can sell all the plowshares you can supply at twenty-five dollars each—Leese wants fifty of them for his store at Sonoma. Suit you?"

"Splendid!" cried Smith. "But what's the crowd here about?"

"Your ragbag collection." O'Farrell fell to laughing again. "I took away one of the big bundles, out of curiosity, and opened it up. Be damned if it didn't have a lot o' shawls and winter shirts inside—just what these sailors need for the Cape Horn passage! So I gave the stuff away to the men from a Boston ship. Some good clothes in the lot, too."

"Fine," said Smith. "What are you grinning about?"

"Oh, just luck!" O'Farrell winked. "What d'ye think, me lad? One of those fellys found an old wallet in the clothes, with money in it! And another one opened up a little old trinket box that fell to his share, and it had a gold piece in it, and be damned if Brown, at the saloon, didn't give him twenty dollars for it! That crowd will be tearing the house down if you don't get outside quick, to be selling them the pile o' plunder! Make 'em bid for it, lad—mind, now! Make 'em bid, sight unseen! It's fair wild they are!"

Smith looked at the Irishman for a minute. "Why—why— you confounded rascal, you!" He broke into laughter.

It was a wild, tumultuous assembly. Smith was seized and mounted on one of the boxes.

"Easy, now, boys," he pleaded. "You want buy this stuff?"

A roar of assent went up.

"All right, then quiet down!" yelled Smith. "Listen, boys! I don't know what's in this stuff. If you buy it, then it's at your own risk—"

"Go on, sell it!" shouted a voice. "What's your price?"

"Make your own price," retorted Smith. "That bundle over there—who wants it? Bid up! Start it at five dollars—"

"Six!" came a yelp. "Eight! It's mine for ten! Fifteen and be damned to you!" The voices stormed. Smith got things under control, and sold the bundle for thirty dollars. A box came next. Here was Leidesdorff, roaring his head off to buy a huge packing case. Here was the Frenchman, Vioget, frantically bidding in a bundle. Officers from the ships, seamen, merchants—the auction was a riot, no less.

One of the boxes was torn to pieces on the spot and yielded kitchenware and some excellent bedding and blankets. These were hard to get in Yerba Buena, and were resold on the instant. Alcalde Bartlett came along, trying to restore order, and catching the general infection fell to bidding on a box, and got it, amid huge laughter.

"Congratulations, Abel."

"Oh!" he said. "Hello, Frank! I suppose you want to check up on the books and get rid of me for good. Well, I'll be over at the store pretty quick."

"I didn't come for that." Ward glanced around, then dropped his voice, as he met Smith's gaze. "I tried to see you after that talk we had, but you had skipped out. I felt damned ashamed of myself, for the way I talked that evening. I still do."

"Why—Frank!" Astonished, incredulous, Smith beamed suddenly. "Doggone it, you got no call to feel so! I guess you were right in what you said—or some of it anyhow."

Ward regarded him gravely. "You have no hard feelings, after the way I trimmed you?"

"Well, Frank, it made me feel bad, sure," said Smith frankly. "But hard feelin's? No. I guess I just couldn't have hard feelin's against you."

The warmth in Ward's face, the sudden leap of emotion in his eyes, was stunning.

"The store isn't the same place without you, Abel." Ward put out his hand. "Will you forgive what I said, and forget it, and

come on back? Make it full partners this time. I guess I've
learned my lesson."

Smith seized the extended hand and gripped it hard, and
held it.

"Frank—why, darn it all—I'm the happiest man in California!" he said huskily.

"No you're not, dammit. I am." Ward's face lit up. "Look,
Abel! You can do any durned thing you please and I'll not say
a word. You can give your Yankee notions their head, savvy?
I've sure learned something; and that is, I can't get on without
you. You and me have to stick together. Is it a deal?"

"You bet," gulped Abel Smith. "I—durn it, I feel the same
way! And if you want, I'll chuck that whale oil and the plowshares smack into the bay."

"Not much," said Ward, with a wry smile. "If I'd had any
sense, I'd have known that you were right about the oil. I've
found out so, anyhow. Come on, even if it's against your principles—let's go over to Brown's and have a drink."

"Principles be damned!" said Abel Smith happily. "Yes, sir,
principles be damned! Come on!"

V

A CHANGE OF NAME

January 27, 1847 Yerba Buena Dies and
San Francisco Was Born—to the No Small
Profit of Abel Smith of Nantucket

ABEL SMITH, junior partner in Ward & Smith, general merchants of Yerba Buena, was a keenly worried young man. Everybody was young here, and youth takes its troubles hard. The only really old man in town was Captain Leidesdorff, who was thirty-five.

Smith had worked his way out to unknown California aboard a Nantucket whaler and joined the band of exiles who lived here in the cove on San Francisco bay. He had made his way, but anybody could do that in Yerba Buena—Good Herb, so named because of the wild mint that grew everywhere. It was a sprawling, scattered little town of eighty houses, but Abel Smith was confident that it would grow. California had been taken over by the United States, the great western emigration was under way, and Yerba Buena had a future. Yet, in this winter of 1846-7, things were looking bad for the town.

On a dark January evening, Smith shut up the store and started home. He was living with the Brannans of Clay Street, and getting there was an adventure. The rains had been heavy. The streets, mere sandy wastes in summer, were now seas of mud. Smith struck a mud-hole, floundered in above his knees, floundered out, and a minute later floundered into another. He cursed heartily.

"Hey! Gimme a hand!" said a husky voice. "I've hollered till I'm hoarse—"

Smith discerned a figure buried to its middle in the thick

mud. He reached out a hand and after a long struggle managed to get the other man out. Who it was, he did not know. "You'll need a new outfit," he said, as the two of them scraped off mud. "Come around to Ward & Smith's in the morning and get it. I'm Smith."

The other cackled out a curse and a laugh, then moved away without giving his name, and heaped upon the town of Yerba Buena and its mudholes some eloquent profanity. Abel Smith, true to Yankee form, had put in a good word for business, and now went onto his destination and supper.

Sam Brannan, who had brought out a shipload of Mormons to settle in the California wilds, was a gay, ruthless, magnetic personality, a soldier of fortune. He and his wife Ann Eliza liked young Smith, as most people did; this young fellow with the blue eyes and friendly air and whip-keen brain had few enemies.

"You look worried, Abel," said Sam, during supper. "Had a row with Frank Ward?"

"No chance of that," Smith replied. "He's a grand fellow. But he wants to buy me out and keep the store himself."

"No! Why, you've built the firm up to what it is!" said Ann Eliza.

"Oh, everything's friendly," Smith explained. "But Frank is thinking of going east. He's got a girl waiting for him in New York. He wants to go back and marry her and arrange to get shiploads of merchandise sent out here regularly, and so forth. It's no question of money. I'd get more than I ever saw in one lump before. But what would I do with it? I'd have to find some business of my own."

"I could find you a dozen things in ten minutes," Brannan said truthfully. He was full of schemes. He had started a newspaper, was running two flour mills, and had a dozen irons in the fire—all going well. Not to mention politics.

Yerba Buena was in a furious boil of politics. Still running Mexican style, the town was ruled by Bartlett as alcalde, or

combination mayor-magistrate. The heavy rains, the lack of present business or any amusement except hard drinking, had made tempers short. Feuds had sprung up everywhere. Captain Leidesdorff, the chief merchant and leading figure in Yerba Buena, enjoyed a fight and fought with everyone in sight.

"I hear Judge Bartlett is going to be investigated," Brannan went on, grinning.

"Who's going to do it?" Smith asked. The territory was under military rule for the moment, Governor Mason at Monterey being in supreme command.

"Mason's getting Leidesdorff to do it. Boy, won't that be rich!"

Brannan chuckled. "They'll be cat and dog, sure enough. Hey, what you rushing your supper for?"

"Got to go out again, durn it," Smith replied. "I've got some of Leidesdorff's paper we took in today, and promised Frank I'd see the Captain about it tonight. Might not be good."

"Yeah, you and Leidesdorff get on pretty good."

"He gave me my start when I landed here," Smith said. "And I like him."

"I don't," said Sam. "Durned old blow-hard. He's got his fingers gripped into everything in town. Some day he'll die poor from over-reaching."

"And you'd like to get your fingers into some of his pies," said Ann Eliza, with a wink at Abel Smith. Sam subsided.

"I hear Larkin's in town," Smith commented presently. "I'd like to meet that man. Richest man in California, they say, and the most influential too."

"Huh!" Brannan snorted. "T. O. Larkin's been here a spell; smart Yankee like you, Abel. He settled at Monterey, became U. S. Consul, and made friends with the greasers. Owns half the country, they say—well, maybe not that much, but plenty. Ain't the kind who makes friends, though."

True enough. Most men here were out for their own interests, and would cut any throat in sight; hence the political fight, which was savage. Bartlett was out to enforce the law and had stepped on numerous toes doing so; a former Navy man, he was scrupulously honest and independent.

"Anyhow," concluded Brannan, "there's no future in this place. Only ships come here. The big wagon trains that are coming across the plains end up at Sutter's fort on the Sacramento. That's the place for a boom, you bet! Next summer there'll be thousands of emigrants heading in there. I'm going up next week and look it over. May open a store there. How about trying it, Abel?"

Smith shook his head. "Thanks. Maybe, but not right now. I'm stuck on this place."

Why? He wondered, as he struggled to make his way back downtown to Leidesdorff's little house. It was not the climate, certainly. Perhaps it was the ocean. Yerba Buena had salt in its air and kept him on his toes. Captain Leidesdorff had ever contended that it would be the great city of the future.

THE LITTLE cove on which the town was built was a mud-flat at low tide, and the water was never more than a foot or two deep. Yet, in the haphazard original survey of the town this cove had been divided up into lots along with the rest. There was no wharf; any boats must land at a rocky point on the north side of the cove. The only road out of town led southward to Santa Clara; the sea and bay cut off the place on three sides. It certainly took optimism to see any future in Yerba Buena.

Smith found Captain Leidesdorff alone, finishing his dinner.

"Ha! I'm glad to see you. Sit down," bellowed the lusty Danish mulatto, whose quarter-deck voice could be heard across the bay. "Accacio! Bring hot coffee."

The Indian boy fetched coffee, a box of Manila cigars was opened, and Leidesdorff beamed on his visitor and examined the drafts that Smith produced. There was practically no money in Yerba Buena. Chits, drafts, personal notes of exchange passed current for cash.

"All correct. Now shut the doors and sit down. I want to talk with you," said the burly captain. Smith complied, and lighted his cigar. "I am in trouble."

"So am I," said Smith, and the other roared with mirth.

"Good! We'll help each other out. Larkin is here and is pushing his scoundrelly plan to ruin me and Yerba Buena. He has influence and friends."

SMITH NODDED. Larkin had formed a grandiose scheme, in concert with Don Mariano Vallejo, who owned wide leagues of land to the north, and others. Vallejo put up the land for a great city on the north shores of the bay; this city was to be named Francesca, after Vallejo's wife. Larkin was to publicize it. All the world had heard of San Francisco Bay. The city was bound to boom. Ships would come there instead of here, and Yerba Buena would wither and perish.

"I thought I showed you a way out," said Smith. Leidesdorff nodded.

"Yes. Change the name of Yerba Buena to San Francisco— ah, a wonderful idea! That would knock Larkin's scheme into a cocked hat. But how to do it? There's the rub! The only way it could be done would be for the alcalde, Judge Bartlett, to issue the order. Have you spoken to anyone else about it—even a whisper?"

"Not a whisper, Captain," said Smith.

"Good! Well, I cannot mention the matter to Bartlett, damn him! I am in a big fight with him. I have been appointed to investigate his handling of city funds; I am going to crush him, understand? I am going to teach him a lesson!"

Leidesdorff went on to breathe fire and fury, with rumbling curses in Danish, French and English. Smith intervened.

"Look, Captain. Why not let Bill Howard, or Frank Ward, handle the matter with Judge Bartlett?"

"Ach, no!" Leidesdorff calmed down. "I dare not breathe the idea to a soul, boy! You know what would happen? Everybody would object. Larkin or his friends would hear of it, and then good night! No, no, I am too smart for that. The name would have to be changed all of a sudden, before anyone suspected it. Only if I were friendly with Bartlett, could that be managed. Maybe, if I crush him and he is removed, and another alcalde appointed, it could be done."

"Doesn't look to me like you were so smart."

"Eh?" Leidesdorff drew down his bushy brows in a questioning stare of surprise. "Me not smart? Why not?"

"Well, not so very." Smith went on in his calm, slow way. "Maybe you can crush Bartlett, but will that do you any good? You know in your heart he's an honest man—"

"Honest?" The captain began to foam again. "He made me move my stuff off the beach! He claimed my warehouse .was occupying city property!"

"And so it was. Now look: if your committee of investigation cleared him of all charges, if you made friends with him again, it might do you a lot of good. That would put him under obligations to you. And then he might be glad to do what you want and change the town's name to San Francisco."

"Hm! Impossible to make friends with him. He won't even speak to me on the street," growled Leidesdorff. "The man is stubborn. He is my enemy. He goes out of his way to persecute me, to accuse me of things! Your idea is good, yes, but it won't work."

"You might be surprised to find yourself mistaken," Smith argued. "Right now, Bartlett is everybody's target. They all want him to give away city property and he won't; he's on the level. If he found you were not his enemy but his friend, he'd be tickled pink! Suppose I have a word with him in the morning, Captain. It won't hurt anything."

"Hm! Well, you are smart; go ahead, you Yankee. But don't mention San Francisco!"

"Trust me for that, Captain."

"And see here. If you can manage it for me, I—well, I'll make you a present of five good city lots."

Smith smiled faintly. City lots, which cost from sixteen to twenty-six dollars each, were a drug on the market. Leidesdorff had lots by the dozen.

"You need not turn up your nose," said the other, sagely. "My boy, some day those lots will be worth a fortune. I tell you this will become the greatest city on this West Coast, maybe the greatest in the world. That is, if Larkin does not kill the place, blast him!"

"I think you can handle Larkin."

"Hm! Maybe. But you said that you were worried, boy. Well, what about?"

ABEL SMITH knew that this blustering man, so lion-like in his fury, was actually soft of heart and honest to a fault. He did not hesitate to set forth his own perplexities and to ask counsel.

"If I sell out to Frank Ward, as he wants," he concluded, "it'll leave me at loose ends. I don't want just a job. I want to get ahead."

Leidesdorff ruminated. "If he buys you out, you'll have money, plenty of money."

"Credit, you mean. Yes."

"Buy city lots with it and sit tight."

"I've got to live."

"Yes. And you are tied up with that Brannan. I tell you, that fellow is a rascal! He is false to everything. Wait and see! However, come in with me, and I will be glad to let you handle business deals for me! You're honest. You're smart."

"I want to be in business for myself," objected Smith.

"All right I'll tell you." Leidesdorff laid a forefinger along his big nose. "You know how to do things. All right, do them! Buy and sell, all kinds of deals, land and wheat and lumber!"

Smith's eyes widened. "That's an idea, for sure!"

"Still, I like city lots," said Leidesdorff, chewing at his cigar. "A lot of people here would like to get out cheap, on account of Larkin's new city; they would gladly sell. But who will buy? I have all I can handle myself. I am saving my money to build a wharf, a fine big wharf to go across the shallow cove and out to deeper water!"

"Those water lots in the cove ought to be worth money, then."

"Maybe, some day; waterfront property, my boy, is always the best. If this town grows, the cove will all be filled in some day. But you go into business for yourself. I can give you more than one deal to handle for me, on the side. So can others."

Something to that, thought Abel Smith, as he adventured homeward through bogs and mud. He was doing this very thing for the firm right now, buying here and selling there; why not for himself?

On the following morning, Judge Washington Bartlett sat in the alcalde's office, very angry and very worried. Sam Brannan's newspaper had just come out with a savage attack on him. Enemies had sprung up everywhere. They were trying to force him to resign, and utterly false charges of fraud were being made against him. He was not afraid of any investigation; he could fight for his principles and did so, without fear. But be was afraid of treachery and lying opponents and traps laid to catch him.

He looked up and nodded, his face clearing, as Abel Smith walked in.

"Morning, Abel, morning to you," he said. "You're about early."

"Well, Judge, I just dropped in for a minute." Smith, invited to a chair, made himself comfortable. The alcalde's stern, wiry features relaxed. This young Yankee took no share in the bitter fights that swept the town, was a friend to everyone, and was known for his smartness and friendliness. A hard worker, too.

"Anything on your mind, Abel?"

"I was sort of looking for advice, Judge. I had a notion about buying maybe one or two city lots, you see."

Bartlett smiled. "Well, the only plat of the city there is, hangs back of the bar down at Brown's saloon. Have you picked out any special lots?"

"No. That's what I wanted to ask you about. I was talking to Captain Leidesdorff last night," said Smith, not missing the swift contraction of Bartlett's lips at the name, "and he allowed your advice would be the best to follow."

"What!" Bartlett let down his chair legs with a bang. "Leidesdorff said that about me? You're joking."

Smith looked at him with wide and innocent gaze.

"Huh? No, I'm not. He did say that you seemed to dislike him and hate him, and he was mighty sorry for it; but he told me you were about the only honest man in town and I could depend on whatever you said about those lots."

BARTLETT'S FACE was a study. He was amazed and gratified and incredulous.

"That's funny. I don't dislike Leidesdorff at all," he said. "His warehouse encroached on city-owned property and I made him move it; he got blazing mad about it, but there was nothing I could do. I think the Captain's a fine fellow, in his way."

"Well, he said the same about you, Judge. I remember, he said that he meant to show up one man who could stand up for his principles, among all these sharks and selfish-minded rascals—he didn't mention any names, but he was talking about you."

Bartlett, with the coming investigation in mind, actually beamed.

"I'm glad to hear that, mighty glad!" he said. "What is it you want to know about the lots?"

Smith talked real estate with him for a while, then departed. He went out of his way to drop in at Leidesdorff's store, and found the captain just arrived.

"Ever in New England, Captain?" he inquired.

"Who, me? I been every place but there, boy. Why?"

"Well, we used to say that you can catch flies with molasses, but not with vinegar," said Smith, and winked. "I just had a word with the alcalde. He spoke mighty well of you."

With this, he went on to his own work, chuckling. Captain Leidesdorff, he knew, could take a hint.

Frank Ward had not yet shown up at the store. Smith got the place open and lit a fire in the stove. The air was thick with fog, and rain would probably come at any ime, and a fire was more than welcome, besides taking the dampness out of the stock. Having swept out, Smith was putting things in shape when a customer entered, a stranger, a tall, slim man, older than most of those around, and quite dignified.

"Good morning," said the stranger. "I'm looking for a Mr. Smith."

"That's me," said Smith, curious as to whom this might be. The stranger put out his hand.

"Glad to meet you, sir. My name is Larkin—of Monterey. I'm the man you pulled out of the mud last night."

Laughing, Smith shook hands heartily. Larkin, however, did not laugh.

"I would be greatly obliged to you, sir," he said, "if you would say nothing of that incident to your friends. It would be most unfortunate, in some ways, if the fact became known that Thomas O. Larkin had been stuck in Yerba Buena mud and damned near suffocated by it! Do you get me?"

Smith nodded quietly. He understood perfectly. On the point of dignity, Larkin was highly touchy. And the story would certainly hold him up to ridicule.

"You may depend on me, Mr. Larkin," he said. "I can keep my mouth shut. I'm a Yankee like you."

At this, Larkin smiled. "Good! And now, young man, I want to reward you for your helping hand, and make sure that you will profit by discretion in the matter." He held out a folded paper. "Here are five excellent lots in the new city on the straits, up north, which I have put in your name. Hang on to them; they should be worth a small fortune some day. That city is the coming metropolis of all California, Mr. Smith. Good day, sir."

Larkin walked out.

Smith's first impulse was to reject the proffered reward; he quickly stiffed the impulse. Actually, he perceived, Larkin was not so much rewarding him as paying him for his silence about the incident. Ridicule was the one thing that the astute Monterey merchant could not stomach—and what a howl would go up and down the state, at the story of T. O. Larkin mired in Yerba Buena mud to his armpits!

"The dignity of wealth is a wonderful thing," reflected Smith,

as he pocketed the deed to the five lots in the city of Francesca. "Worth a fortune, eh? Not much."

He smiled at thought of Captain Leidesdorff's plans to blow
Francesca higher than a kite. If ever the name of Yerba Buena
were changed to San Francisco—then goodbye to the booming
city on the straits! Not all of Larkin's influence could save it.
But, until that change of name came to pass and the captain's
secret plans revealed, the cards were certainly stacked against
Yerba Buena.

Abel Smith, who was good at keeping his mouth shut, said
nothing to anyone of his meeting with T. O. Larkin.

As the days passed, he became more occupied with his own
troubles. Those of the town factions swirled around him unob-
served. The investigating committee headed by Captain Leidesdorff was going after Judge Bartlett hot and heavy, it was said.
Bets were freely placed as to the outcome; Yerba Buena was
going in more and more for gambling of all kinds, but chiefly
monte, and games were running day and night in every saloon
and hotel. Both saloons and hotels were highly primitive affairs
of course but liquor was sold and beds were rented to justify
the names.

Abel Smith was grieved at the thought of dissolving partnership. The name of Ward & Smith meant a lot to him. A partnership in a going and growing business, a prosperous one, had
been a big thing and still was, in his eyes. This meant more than
the money. He would not lose financially, but he would be out
on his own again.

FRANK WARD was extremely friendly, of course, but his
position was understandable and quite definite. He wanted to
bring his bride from the East, and he wanted to show off before
her as a merchant who owned his own business; that was
natural. Ward was well off financially and had put money into
numerous projects.

"I'll hate to see that sign come down, Frank," said Abel

Smith, when at length the issue came into the open and had to be settled.

"So will I, Abel," Ward replied. "But I'll need to draw in my horns a bit, with a wife to provide for. How would it be if I paid you in part with bills on the firm, which you can use as cash, and in part with other things? For instance, I have a number of town lots, and some up in Francesca as well. Larkin's new city, you know."

"Francesca lots? What'd I do with 'em?"

Ward laughed. "Well, you can always sell 'em to Kanaka Davis. Grimes & Davis are in cahoots with Larkin, you know. I took a dozen of those lots at rock bottom, and Davis would be glad to take 'em off my hands. Or, if you like, there's the little redwood house on Clay Street that I took in on a deal with Leidesdorff. I don't need it. I'm getting a bigger one built before I get back from the East."

"Tell you what you do, Frank," said Smith. "You want me out; all right, I'll get out. Now, you're on the square. You go ahead and figure what the partnership is worth, and how you want to pay it—the redwood house, the lots and so forth. If there's no definite reason against it, I'll abide by whatever you say. Is that fair?"

"So fair that I'll not hold you to it," Ward replied. "We're friends, and we'll always be friends, I hope. I'll draw up the paper and you look it over. Say, in a couple days. No hurry."

Smith nodded agreement.

Bleakly, he cast about for some other occupation, and found nothing; opportunities lacked in Yerba Buena. With the arrival of the U. S. naval squadron, bluejackets and marines had money to spend. Out by the old mission, two miles south of town, there were bull fights and other amusements of a Sunday, but except for the ships that came in, Yerba Buena saw little spending, being cut off by water from the country around. The town was growing, but slowly.

Accacio, Leidesdorff's Indian servant, summoned him one

afternoon to the captain's house. When Smith got there, Leidesdorff closed the doors, poured drinks and opened a box of cigars,
seeming highly pleased with himself.

"My boy, it is all fixed, thanks to you," he said, beaming.

"You mean, with Bartlett?"

"Aye. The investigation will exonerate him; we are friends
again. He is a fine man. I like him. And—listen!" Finger along
nose, Leidesdorff winked. "On the 27th, he issues the order as
alcalde. We become San Francisco. And not a soul suspects it!
Drink!"

Abel Smith seldom drank, but the enormous gusto of his
host forced him to it now.

"There is something you can do for me." Leidesdorff rubbed
his big hands enjoyably. "I told you to go in business for yourself—ha! Now, this Kanaka Davis, of Grimes & Davis, is an
obstacle. Those fellows are friends of Larkin; he has an interest
in their business. They do not like me."

"Meaning you don't like them," said Smith shrewdly. The
other roared with laughter.

"Maybe, maybe! Well, I am going to build another hotel;
we'll need it by summer, when ships from the East begin to
come in. Kanaka Davis owns two lots that I must have to fill
out the site. I own the rest. These are in Block 3 of the city plat.
You buy them for me."

"Why don't you do it for yourself?"

"That scoundrel would charge me terrible prices if he thought
I wanted them! I know the rascal. They cost him sixteen dollars
each. You get hold of them for me. I must have them for the
new hotel, you comprehend? I will give you a good profit on
whatever you pay for them. That is what I mean by doing business for yourself, my boy. You see?"

Smith nodded. "And you promised me five lots for myself,
if the change of name went through."

"That is right. I keep my promises."

Abel Smith went away thoughtfully. He had thought up and

engineered this whole scheme for changing the town's name, that meant so much to Leidesdorff and others; in return, he would get five lots worth about eighty dollars. That sort of business was not profitable, he told himself. The 27th was only a week away, too.

He did not hurry to see Kanaka Davis; this same evening, he was to talk business with Frank Ward, and it filled his thoughts. He met Ward after supper and they went into the deal.

He was somewhat astonished by Ward's generosity. The price to be paid him was really respectable; he had never owned so much money at once in his life. This, of course, would not be money, but its equivalent. A dozen lots in Francesca, ten more here in town, the redwood cottage and a good sum in due bills on the firm.

Smith agreed; he was unhappy about it, though not about the price. The dissolution of partnership papers were all drawn up and ready. He signed them. He shook hands with Ward and had a drink to their future, and it was done. He went out into the night dejected and morose, feeling as though he had not a friend in the world.

NEXT MORNING he slept late, then went downtown. The news had already spread around. Everybody asked what he was going to do, and he had no answer. There were plenty of things to do, if he wanted a job; but he wanted more than this. He had no great confidence in Leidesdorff's suggestion of handling any sort of deal for himself. At last, recollecting the business in hand, he headed for Grimes & Davis.

Kanaka Davis was a pleasant, efficient, hard-eyed man who had tangled with Abel Smith once or twice previously and turned up his nose at Yankee smartness. They were friendly enough, however.

"I hear you're out of the firm," said Davis. "You and Frank Ward have a row?"

"Not a bit of it," Smith rejoined brightly. "He just wanted to have the whole thing, so I got out. I don't know yet what I'll do."

"Won't do much here, I guess. This town is done for."

"You're crazy, Davis! You just wait till summer. The boom will start then, maybe before then."

"Nope, she's as good as finished," Davis said firmly. "Me, I'm putting my money on Larkin's new town up the straits."

"Francesca? Well, I dunno." Smith hesitated. "I've got some lots up there, and I took in some more from Frank as part payment of our partnership, but—"

"Want to sell 'em?" snapped Davis, bright eyes eager.

"I don't aim to give 'em away," said Smith. "They're good lots."

"How about a swap?" suggested the other. "I got a right smart parcel o' lots here in town."

"Hm! Might be," said Smith reflectively. "Depends on what you got to offer. I don't want any sandlots, blocks away from the Plaza in the swamps!"

With seventeen Francesca lots to dispose of, he discussed prices and locations with Davis, and finally arranged an even swap, lot for lot. An hour later they met at the alcalde's office, signed up the papers, and Abel Smith found himself owner of two lots in Block 3 and fifteen other pieces of local property. Kanaka Davis was so highly pleased with the deal, convinced as he was that Yerba Buena was a gone coon, that he bought a drink with unexampled generosity.

During the next couple of days, Abel Smith did what he had never before done—nothing. He just hung around town making a nuisance of himself and keeping eyes and ears wide open. To his own surprise, he found a number of things to which he could turn his hand, and usually at a profit. Some wanted advice, some wanted definite help with a problem, consignments of goods were unwelcome here, welcome there. He was not hungry for gain, gave a helping hand freely, and in consequence was a much sought-after person. This pleased as well as surprised him.

For the first time, he began to gain confidence in his own ability to handle any sort of deal that might turn up.

Incidentally, he ran into a number of men who had invested in Yerba Buena town lots, and who now regretted it, in view of the fact that the new city up the straits was going to kill Yerba Buena deader than a door nail. It was no great trick to allow himself to be saddled with these properties, either on long-term agreements or for due bills on Frank Ward. His supply of these latter was shrinking, and his holdings' in Yerba Buena lots were growing to astonishing proportions, when on the afternoon of the 26th he ran into Captain Leidesdorff.

"Hey! I want to see you, young feller!" bellowed the captain. "Come along with me."

SMITH DUTIFULLY followed the captain home. Cigars and drinks were set forth, the doors were shut, and Leidesdorff fastened a murky eye upon him.

"Out with it, my boy, out with it! Did you see Kanaka Davis?"

"Oh, sure," said Smith.

"Well? What about it? Did you get those lots in Block 3?"

"Oh, those! Yes, I bought them from him."

"Ha! Good! Dig up the deeds and sign 'em over," said the captain gleefully. "I'll give you a ten percent commission on the deal."

Smith studied his cigar-end.

"You know, Captain," he said in his mild way, "that tomorrow Alcalde Bartlett is going to issue that order—eh?"

"Yes. It's all made out and signed. To be made public tomorrow. And," added the captain with relish, "won't there be hell to pay! And nothing anybody can do about it."

"That'll be fine," said Smith. "I figure that the minute this town becomes San Francisco, the value of property here is going to get good and firm and stay firm."

"Firm? That's no name for it!" boomed Leidesdorff. "You're

going to see sixteen-dollar lots worth thousands when the boom comes!"

Smith nodded. "I hope so. That's why I'd sooner hang onto those lots in Block 3 for myself, Captain. It's a good location."

Leidesdorff turned purple. His language beggared reproduction.

"Why—why—you damned Yankee trickster!" he gasped out when be could manage coherent speech. "You snake! You blackguard! You got those lots for me!"

"For myself, Captain. You advised me to go into business for myself—"

"And I trusted you! Blast your blasted hide, I'll break you for this trick!" foamed the other, pounding the table with his fist. "You know why I want those lots. You know I have to have them for my new hotel!"

"They're mine," said Abel Smith mildly. "They're going to be valuable, Captain, but I'll give you a ten-year lease on them."

"Lease? A lease?" roared the captain furiously.

"Sure. I'm tired of living around like I am. I'll turn over a lease and you can go ahead and build your hotel. In return, you guarantee me room and board at the hotel for the length of the lease—isn't that fair? You know I wouldn't hold you up, Captain. I don't want a red cent out of you."

Leidesdorff puffed out his cheeks. The fury died gradually from his eyes.

"Ten years! Why not fifty, a hundred?"

"I'm not sure whether San Francisco will be here that long, or me either," Smith replied, a faint twinkle in his blue eyes. "I'll settle for ten."

"You Yankee devil, you!" A tincture of admiration crept into Leidesdorff's voice. "And suppose, after ten years, that I'm not here—that a huge, growing city is here—and those two lots revert to you—they'll be worth a fortune!"

"That's what I'm thinking, Captain."

Leidesdorff relaxed. He picked np his forgotten cigar and puffed it alive. Suddenly he put it down again and a bellow of laughter escaped him.

"Done with you, done with you!" he gasped. "Boy, I like you—damme if I, don't! Go into business for yourself, I said—and you've done it! You've done it! All right. The deal is made. Yes, sir, you're in business for yourself, sure enough!"

"At least I've started," said Abel Smith.

And on the morrow, January 27, 1847, by ukase of Alcalde Bartlett, Yerba Buena died and San Francisco was born. To the no small profit of Abel Smith of Nantucket.

VI

"GOLD!"... IS WHERE YOU FIND IT!

ABEL SMITH of Nantucket—they called him that, to distinguish him from the other Smiths—was not doing any too well, and had to admit it. Not openly, of course; only to Justine, who was a waitress at John Henry Brown's hotel.

Justine Finch had come overland with a wagon-train of emigrants, but her folks had died and she drifted in to San Francisco an orphan of eighteen. Women were mighty scarce here in this winter of 1847-8, and Justine could have been married a hundred times over; instead, she went to work at the hotel, and the salt air put new bloom in her cheeks. She had a good level head, which was why Abel Smith took to her in the first place. Before the end of the winter he was going with her steadily, to the fury of many other men.

There were over a hundred houses in town now, three times that number of residents, and Smith firmly believed that San Francisco had a big future. He had worked his way out to California aboard a whaler, and had prospered here as clerk and partner in a store, but for nearly a year he had been nosing out business for himself, and business had nosed him out to an alarming extent.

"I'm not broke," he confided to Justine .one evening, as they walked along the beach of the cove on which the town stood, "but I'm getting pretty badly bent. One deal after another has gone wrong. I dunno when we'll get that farm and settle down and get married, Justine; looks farther away all the time."

"Never mind, Abel; we can wait a while," she rejoined, pulling the shawl about her shoulders, for the late winter night was chill. "Maybe you'd better go to work for some store again. There's an awful lot of smart men around here in competition with you."

"Not me. I'm going to make good working for myself, or go bust," Smith rejoined stubbornly. "I'm just as smart as they are, and I aim to prove it. Only, I want to go to farming, and there's no future for farming in California. All they do is raise cattle. All they produce is hides and tallow. Justine, as soon as I begin to make money instead of lose it, as soon as we have a farm—"

"Then we'll get married," she finished, as he paused.

"And you'll go to the bullfight and fandango out at the old mission, on Sunday, with me?"

She grimaced. "No. I don't like bullfights, Abel. And I half-promised Jasper O'Farrell I'd go with him to the fandango."

He looked at her, shocked. "You did? Why? You like him better than me?"

"Of course not, but he asked me first, didn't he?" she said practically. "If you're there I'll save you most of the dances, though."

The evening ended badly for Abel Smith. He was young; everyone in San Francisco was young. O'Farrell, who had roved all over Mexico and South America, was only twenty-four. He had recently surveyed the town—a wild, happy-go-lucky young Irishman whom everyone liked. Even Abel Smith liked him, at times.

No, business was plentiful, but it had gone against Smith of late. Over-confidence, of course. It had looked easy, and it was easy, to swing deals here and there. With thirty or forty ships lying in the enormous bay, with saloons and stores making money hand over fist, with houses at high premium in this rainy season, Abel Smith had plenty to do; but the flyers he took failed to fly of late.

Chiefly his dream of a farm had failed him, at heavy loss. It was a nice piece of property; but the American occupation, a year and a half ago, had uncovered quite a few fraudulent titles, and this was one of them. So, as February wore into March, Abel Smith of Nantucket licked his wounds and his New England caution postponed any notion of getting married too hastily.

SUNDAY FOUND him in no holiday mood. He lived at John Henry Brown's hotel, and on Sundays the hotel was a madhouse—the bar running full tilt, gambling rooms roaring, and Doc Leavenworth preaching, all at once. With men ashore from the ships in port and everybody in town on holiday bent, Smith was lonely. He seldom drank, the bullfights at the old mission two miles down the road had no allure for him, and most of his friends happened to be out of town. Financially, he was far from broke, but had sunk most of his available funds in city lots and had lost the remainder in his farm venture. With the hotel dining room running full blast all day long, Justine had no time for him; hence, the world looked gloomy.

He had no interest in gambling, except on his own judgment, but he watched the monte games that afternoon just for the pleasure of seeing cash. Real money was almost unknown here—paper served its purpose well enough—but the troops and the Navy men on the station were paid in cash, and so were the ships' crews that flocked in, so it gravitated to the saloons and monte games.

Big, genial Bill Howard, and the spruce New Yorker, Frank Ward, were having a business confab in one corner. Both were merchants; Ward had been Abel Smith's partner in a store, until he bought Smith out a year ago, and was hoping to get away for the east to marry a girl he had left behind him. Howard crooked a finger at Smith, who joined them and pulled up a chair.

"Here's a chance for your Yankee wits, Abel," said Ward. "Howard & Mellus are going to expand, going to open stores at Sonoma and maybe at Sutter's Fort. Tell him about it, Bill. He can do it if anyone can."

Howard nodded in his amiable way. He was easy-going and well liked everywhere.

"Might be. Commission in it, anyhow. Your friend Sam Brannan is up at Sutter's now, Abel, opening a store. We aim to do likewise. First, we'll need a couple fifty-ton launches or schooners to run up the Sacramento from here. Our funds are all tied up; we've got a five-hundred acre strip on the Cosumne River, a fine big flat, that we got stuck with last fall, and we want to figure some way of turning it into the boats we need."

"Is it a ranch?" Smith asked.

The others grinned. "So-called. Couple log shacks on it, anyhow. You know as well as we do that land's worthless around here."

This, in a sense, was so. While under Mexican rule, anyone could get grants of land in enormous quantities for nothing; it was measured by the square mile rather than by the acre. Now that California had been taken over by the United States, land still had small actual value, especially on the numerous rivers that poured down from the Sierras.

Howard hauled out some papers. "Here's a detailed description of the property, Abel, if you want to try and turn the deal. The main thing is not to let anyone know that we need the boats; we want to keep it dark about starting a store upriver, until spring. But we must have those two launches."

Smith glanced over the papers. "You'll swap the property for the boats?"

"Sure as shooting."

"Then you'd better deed it to me so I can handle the deal if a chance offers, without dragging you into it."

This was fair enough, and Bill Howard was glad to do it. Business deals and even property rights were loosely and trustingly handled in that day. There was not a thief in the whole land, and anyone like Abel Smith was so well known that his word was as good as his bond.

"Any time limit on this?" he asked. "How long will you give me to swing it?"

"Oh, suit yourself," Howard replied. "February's about out—say, the end of March? If we pick up a couple of boats before then, go ahead and get rid of the property for whatever you can get; otherwise, swap it for rivercraft and nothing else."

Things were happening up those inland waters even now, but Abel Smith was far from suspecting it. Neither was anyone else aware of it.

THE FIFTY-TON craft known locally as launches, were the chief means of communication around the bay and up the Sacramento; and they were not easily come by. Smith knew that a number were owned around the bay, and had some hope of turning the desired deal, one way or another.

When he read over the description of that five hundred acres, however, it made his mouth water. The Cosumne was just below

Sutter's place on the American, and his first thought was that here must be the very farming land of his dreams. Then, as he read farther, he shook his head. No; this was good cattle land, but rocky and poor for farming, badly broken up by dry gulches and ravines. It was, in fact, good for absolutely nothing.

That evening he toiled two miles out to the old mission through the mud and got there to see O'Farrell and Justine having a grand time. He did have one dance with Justine but he was in sombre mood and angry at O'Farrell, and sour on the world.

The fandango was gay enough. Half the town was there, and Californians had come in force from the ranches scattered over the peninsula, riding in with all their finery for the week-end fiesta, spreading laughter and smiles and soft Spanish compliments around.

In San Francisco were almost none of these native-born, the town being practically solidly American.

The young man from Nantucket dourly wished he could be carefree and merry as was Jasper O'Farrell, who never worried about anything, never had anything, and yet never lacked for anything. Nor could he remain angry with Jasper; no one could. He voiced a bit of his thoughts, while dancing with Justine, and her dark eyes sparkled at him.

"Never mind, Abel. I prefer you to Jasper any day, and you know it. You have a lot he doesn't have. He's good company for an evening, but life partners is different."

Abel Smith cheered up and told about the commission job he had just taken on. To his surprise, she drew him out of the dance and off to one side, hastily.

"Abel, did you say boats—those big boats that go up to Sacramento and sail across the bay?"

"That's it. Launches," he assented.

"Launches! That's just what he said!" Her eyes flashed at him. "He said that he wanted to sell them tomorrow, and he had two."

"Who? What? Where?" demanded Abel Smith, scenting game like a bird-dog.

"A man I was waiting on at supper. He came up today from San Jose, that little town down at the foot of the bay. He was talking with John Henry Brown and I heard them—"

"Who was he?" shot out Smith.

She shook her head. "I don't know. But he had a room at the hotel—"

"And John Henry would know him, of course!" Abel Smith caught hold of her and jubilantly hugged her in front of everybody. "Thanks, Justine! You're the kind of a partner that's worth while having—see you tomorrow!"

Whereupon he left her standing there and put for the door, and legged it back for town. This proceeding, naturally, was not calculated to flatter any young lady, but Justine Finch looked after him with a smile on her lips and warmth in her eyes. Perhaps she understood Abel Smith far better than he did himself. Justine had been farm raised anyhow, and was a trifle distrustful of the gallant ways of such suitors as Jasper O'Farrell, who was not the marrying kind.

A B E L   S M I T H disregarded darkness and rnudholes, having at such moments a one-track mind. He got back to town splashed and winded, and lost no time in locating the proprietor, whom he knew very well.

John Henry Brown was a pleasant man who loved to gossip, and also loved to be deeply mysterious about himself and his past in old England. By his own tell, the secret of his birth involved one of the greatest families in the old country, and many a nobleman's son had run away to sea. As a matter of fact he was an amiable, plausible chap who had deserted from a Bristol trader and had carved out his present hotel business from scratch.

He listened to Abel Smith's breathless inquiries, and laughed.

"Oh, I know the fellow you mean—you know him too, Abel. Bill Simons, from San Jose, in the hide and tallow business, or was. Tells me that he's going out of business and means to raise cattle."

"Where is he?"

"Well, I just left him at the bar a couple of minutes ago, so I expect he's still there. You've got a deal on?"

"I hope so. Thanks a lot, John Henry," said Smith, and departed for the bar.

He knew Simons, of course; everyone in this country knew everyone else, within a limited range. A hard, tough old bird was Simons, straight as a string but all of forty. That was old age, hereabouts.

Simons was still at the bar. Abel Smith greeted him, took a Manila cigar instead of the proffered drink—he seldom indulged in liquor—and adroitly managed the talk until he was able to swing it around to the subject of launches. Simons took the bait and growled that he would certainly like to get rid of his own two boats.

Five minutes later they were really talking business. Simons was sick of the hide and tallow business, which was the only export business there was here, and was going in for raising his own cattle over on the San Joaquin, and had a better idea of land than most men hereabouts. Five hundred good acres in exchange for his two launches—but were they good?

"You bet they are," said Smith. "Here's the description. Read it for yourself."

Simons read and nodded. "See here, I know you, Smith. Good reputation for honesty. If you say this land is all right, I'll make the deal. Mind, on your sayso alone."

Abel Smith reflected quickly. Bill Howard would have told him if anything had been wrong with those acres.

"It's all right," he said promptly. "I'll guarantee it. Good land."

"Fine. Done with you." Simons shook hands on the bargain. "Gimme the deed. I'm going back to San Jose tomorrow and I'll have the two boats sailed up here for delivery to you next day."

They went to the visitor's room, wrote out and signed the necessary papers, and Abel Smith found himself owner of the two launches. A nice bit of business, he told himself.

At noon next day, he had lunch with Bill Howard. Anyone less honest than Smith might have tried to turn an extra penny; but he put the deal straight before Howard and deeded over the ownership of the two launches, and pocketed his commission. Howard was pleased, naturally, and admired his swift action in the matter.

"I'll bet that property is under water right now, with the high rains we've had," Howard commented. "Say, that reminds me! I heard from that man Charley Bennett."

"Who?" queried Smith.

"Bennett. Remember him? The fellow who was dead broke, and you staked him to an outfit at the store last fall. Well, he's working for Cap Sutter now and sent word he aimed to pay up what he owed pretty soon. He's helping to build a sawmill for Sutter at Columa, wherever that is."

Abel Smith shrugged and forgot about the man. He forgot about the launch deal, too, after the launches had duly arrived and were found satisfactory. But he did not forget about it very long—merely a matter of a week or so. Then the heavens fell for sure.

Mr. Simons showed up, with blood in his eye and fire on his tongue. He had made a quick trip to inspect his new property, and a quicker trip back home.

"I took over that land on your guarantee, Smith," he said.

"Anything wrong with it?" demanded Abel Smith.

"No. Not a thing, I guess. Only there ain't no land," said the other grimly. "It's two foot under water. Flooded all winter, soon's the rains begin—every winter. Now, I don't aim to be cheated. There's a lot o' things I can do, soon as I go to work on 'em. And on you. What I want to know is whether your sayso is good or not."

Abel Smith was vaguely aware of the gulf yawning under him.

"Of course it's good," he rejoined heatedly. "And you've got no call to say that I cheated you!"

"Then prove up. Take back your cussed no-account land. Gimme my two launches."

"But—I can't! They're sold!"

"You got two hours to make good, or I go to work," said Simons, and meant it.

Abel Smith scurried about frantically. In one sense, of course, a swap was a swap; but he was too honest to deny that he had guaranteed that land as good. If his word was publicized as worthless, his reputation would be ruined and his whole future gone. Nor was he minded to go back on his word. He tried to get the launches back.

Bill Howard sympathized with him, but refused point-blank. The launches were now up the Sacramento. Howard & Mellus had them, and needed them, and meant to keep them.

"I gave you no guarantee," Bill said truthfully. "I hate to see you stuck, but that isn't my fault, Abel. You got to wriggle out of your own hole, I guess."

Desperately, Smith went back to Simons and put all his cards on the table. Luckily, Simons was quick to realize that Abel Smith was honest as daylight; he smoked and ruminated over the matter, and came to decision.

"Tell you what I'll do, Smith. I'll deed that land back to you; it's yours. I'll put a price on the boats—say, four hundred dollars. Fair enough. You raise the money and we'll call it square."

Smith could not raise a tenth part of the money and said so. He might have turned to his old employer and backer, Captain Leidesdorff; but the captain was some forty thousand in debt, and in bed to boot, being down with the sickness that was to finish him ere long. No help there. No help anywhere.

Every cent that Abel Smith could rake and scrape, during the past year or so, had gone into San Francisco lots—fifty-yard

lots at sixteen fifty, one hundred-yard lots at twenty-six dollars.
At those figures, it took a good many lots to tot up four hundred
dollars—so many, indeed, that when he went over the figures
he was aghast. He had bought to hold against the future, being
confident that with the big flood-tide of immigration coming
in by wagon train across the plains, San Francisco was bound
to be a big city.

Borrowing the money was out of the question—there was
no such thing as a bank in the whole country, and borrowing
would leave him no better off anyhow. He would have to sell
his lots outright, and it was worse than pulling teeth. Naturally he could not sell them at any profit whatever, since the
town had plenty more lots to sell at the same prices, and the
boom had not yet started. It would not start until summer, when
the prairie schooners from the east began coming in.

So Abel Smith stood up to the shock, and gulped down his
medicine like a man, though it was a bitter pill indeed. His
New England conscience would not let him do anything else.
He scurried around and managed to sell some of his lots, while
Simons took over others to make up the price of the launches.
Thus the deal was concluded, and Simons went home satisfied.

THAT EVENING Smith conferred with Justine and laid
the whole miserable affair before her. He was heartsick and
wretched. She heard him out, then reached out and took his
hand and patted it comfortingly.

"Never mind, Abel; you did right, aad that's the main thing.
I'm proud of you, I certainly am!"

"Proud of nothing," he rejoined bitterly. "I've struck a hard
streak. A week ago I thought things were bad—but now! I'm
cleaned out, do you realize it? I'm stuck with that strip of worthless land on the Cosumne river. All I have left is five lots here
in town. I saved out the best ones—but that's all."

"Well," said practical Justine, "five town lots will be a good
enough gamble, if this town ever does boom; otherwise, it'll be
small loss. The best of all is that you're honest and everyone

knows it. You're not a smart slicker, like some here I could put a name to. You don't have to be rich, Abel, for us to get married. Land knows, I wouldn't be marrying you for your money."

"Not likely," he said with a harsh laugh. "But I've got to be able to support a wife, when we do."

"Shucks! You can always do that. And, Abel! Since I've been working at the hotel I've got quite a little money laid by. Why don't you take it, or let me lend it to you? I'd be real glad."

He kissed her—an amazing thing to do in that day, when a kiss practically meant marriage; but then, after all, San Francisco was always notably loose in its morals. He laughed and refused the offer.

"Can't do that, sweetheart; I will if I need it, though. We'll get married as soon as I have a farm to bring you to, and not before," he said. "Things are terrible uncertain in this new country. Now I've got to start all over, and I'll do it somehow. I'll figure out a way—you wait and see."

Justine, completely confident in his ability, waited; but for some days Abel Smith's figuring was no more than a row of ciphers.

Worse, the news got out and was quick to spread around. Nobody could have any secrets in this little town at the end of the world. Smith was offered no end of employment, but he was not after a job at all, and refused every offer. Ward would be glad to have him manage the store in which he had formerly been a partner, among others, but it was hard to swallow his pride sufficiently for that.

Jasper O'Farrell, in his generous Irish way, came around not to exult but to offer him partnership in a small ranch up Sonoma way, and very handsomely too.

"No hard feelings, Abel," said he. "I've had it all out with Justine, and you've given me a bad trimming there. She told me as much. So here's my hand and more power to you, me lad, and for her sake I'd be glad to help you if I can."

"Thanks, Jasper," said Abel Smith, warmly grateful. "But I'll make out. I'm not licked—just a run of bad luck. It'll turn around, you'll see."

"Y' know," went on the Irishman, "you ought to get hold of the Galbraith place, near Sonoma. Right nice place of a hundred acres and a jim dandy house. Galbraith went to Sutter's and never did come back—I dunno why. I'd buy that farm myself if I had the money—and the girl."

"I know Galbraith, sure," said Abel Smith. "But I can't be interested in buying farms, Jasper. I may go back to work for Frank Ward."

His confidence in himself was shattered. He could manage the store for Ward, and almost made up his mind to do so, but hung off desperately before deciding, in the hope that something might turn up.

When it did turn up, he was feeling too despondent to care. True, he did not know it was turning up. He heard that Sutter's launch was coming in, and went on about his business with a shrug. It meant nothing to him. Even, later, when he heard that Charley Bennett and Galbraith had come on the launch from the Sacramento, it meant nothing. He had staked Bennett the previous fall, but a few dollars more or less would not matter now.

That evening he ran into both men at the hotel, and shook hands heartily.

"We been looking for you, Abel," said Bennett, with an air of mystery. "Want to have a talk—in private."

"Private, you bet," said Galbraith. Both men had been drinking a bit. "Got to get off in the morning. Going down to Monterey to see Governor Mason."

"Come up to my room if you want to talk," said Smith.

"I'll show you something to bug your eyes out, too," Bennett put in.

They went up to Smith's room, lighted the whale-oil lamp, and settled down with pipes going.

"I hear you got a stretch of land along the Cosumne," said

Galbraith. He winked at Bennett, who was nervous and excited. "How much?"

"Five hundred acres," said Smith. "Say, what you boys got on your mind, anyhow?"

"You hold your hosses," Galbraith rejoined, grinning. "Look, I got a hundred acres fenced, near Sonoma, with a right good house. How'll you swap for your Cosumne land?"

"Quick—if you mean it," said Smith, staring.

Then Bennett broke in. "Hold on, you fellers! Galbraith, Abel done me a good turn last fall. Staked me to clothes and such, when I was dead broke. I aim to pay him back 'fore you git his land off'n him. Now, Abel, looky here."

He took a quinine bottle out of his pocket, then paused, squinting at Smith.

"Swear you won't breathe a word to any living soul?"

"All right, I swear I won't," Smith said with curiosity. "What you got?"

From the bottle, Bennett dumped out on the table a little heap of yellow dust. His eyes were glittering; excitement had hold of him. Smith stirred the dust with his finger.

"Well? What is it?"

"What you think?" whispered Bennett. "We found it on the Columa, where we're building Cap Sutter's sawmill. Marshall, he found it. Sutter has leased the whole durned valley from the Injuns. We're going south to get Governor Mason to okay the lease, see?"

Smith shook his head. "No. I don't see. What is this stuff, anyhow?"

"There's more of it on the Cosumne. That's why Galbraith wants to get your land there. We been there and picked some up."

"Some—what?"

"Gold," breathed Bennett. "Gold, savvy? By gosh, it's all over the place! Once the news gets out, there'll be the biggest damned rush you ever seen! Not a soul but us knows it yet. Now you see why Galbraith wants your land."

Abel Smith was slow to see, slower to believe. Gold? Maybe it was, but nobody had ever heard of gold being picked up. Still, it broke through his reserve as he caught the infectious excitement of the other two men staring at him.

"Gold! So old Cap Sutter has found a gold mine, has he?" he said.

Galbraith cleared his throat. "You better hang on to that land on the Cosumne," he said. "I'm tellin' you, I'd swap in a minute, but there's plenty for all. I ain't greedy. Sutter picked up a chunk big as your thumb!"

Abel Smith took fire and no mistake, but fought back the flames. If this thing were true—good lord! It staggered him, then his brain cleared and he began to see what the discovery might mean. A rush for the Sacramento, sure; everybody in the country would go piling up there to pick up gold. The towns would be empty in no time.

What if Cap Sutter had found a gold mine? Let the other boys lose their heads and go rushing away. There was more than one kind of a gold mine to be found. A little gold flecked in the ground would soon peter out, but wheat crops would not.

"Shucks!" Abel Smith pushed away the yellow dust. "Don't believe a word of it, boys. Maybe someone's been playing a joke on Cap Sutter. Gold? Not likely. Or if it is, then there won't be much of it."

He made it sound convincing, too. The others stared at him angrily.

"Well, I've done my best to square up with you," growled Bennett, scraping up the gold again.

"You have, and you can forget it, Charley," said Abel Smith. "Galbraith, if you want to swap your ranch for my land on the Cosumne river—"

GALBRAITH DID. The deeds were made out and signed and taken downstairs to be witnessed, without delay. The two

departed, anxious to find horses and get off, without even stop-
ping to sleep, so anxious were they to get their errand done and
be back where gold was being picked up.

But Abel Smith went to see Justine. And he was a different
person from the gloomy, morose young man who had been
courting her of late.

"Things are looking up, Justine," he said cheerfully, a new
sparkle in his eye, a new spring to his step. "I'm going to have
that ranch before you can say Jack Robinson!"

"That's grand, Abel!" she returned. "What's happened?"

"So much that I can't begin to tell about it. Anyhow, I swore
to keep quiet. But you offered me what money you had saved
up, a few days ago. Now I'll borrow all you can turn over to me,
if you're still in the mind to let me have it."

Justine laughed and assented eagerly. She had saved up a
nice little sum, too, and Abel Smith was glad to take it.

With morning, he started out to borrow from everyone who
would lend him money, and now he reaped the rewards of a
good reputation. Small sums or large, he took all he could get
from any source; his credit was excellent, and he got plenty on
his word alone.

After that he just kept his mouth shut and did business very
quietly.

A week passed, and another week. Rumors began to fly
around town, heavily discounted. A gold mine? Everybody
jeered at the notion. But the rumors persisted. More, it soon
became known that there was a general movement among the
settlers toward the Sacramento. Fools for their pains, said folks.
Who ever heard of gold being picked up?

More time passed. The rumors became more and more
weighty. Then, one day, into town came Sam Brannan, waving
a yellow bottle and shouting at the top of his lungs. "Gold!
Gold on the Sacramento! Gold!"

He started a stampede, sure enough. But the only way anyone
could reach the Sacramento in a hurry was by boat; and it was

suddenly discovered that all the boats in town were owned or controlled by Abel Smith, who demanded simply outrageous prices for them.

But price was no object, with gold to be picked up. The rush was on. From all the towns and settlers' camps, from the country to the south, men went pouring forth to the Sacramento in maddened flocks. The ships in the harbor were empty. Soldiers and sailors skipped out. San Francisco itself emptied almost overnight until it was a deserted village.

"Me? Not much. Let 'em go and be hanged!" chuckled Abel Smith, as he sat in talk with Justine, and paid back his borrowings with interest. "If there's gold on that land, Galbraith's welcome. Here's the deed to the farm, and it's in your name, my dear."

"Mine? But it's ours! When are we going there, Abel?"

"About the first of June, I reckon," he said. "That suit you?"

Justine plucked at her dress. "I thought you were in a hurry to get married and go to farming?"

"I am," said Abel Smith, frowning. "But—but we'll need money to start with."

"I thought you made a lot in those boats and things you sold?"

"Well, I did; but I sunk it again," he confessed. "I bought some store stocks in cheap; pretty quick, everybody's going to be hollering for food on the Sacramento. And I bought a store, too, from a feller who was in a hurry to get away. And—"

"And some more town lots, I suppose?"

"Oh, one or two, yes. Pretty quick, this is going to be a great city. We won't have long to wait, Justine. Sam Brannan has already offered to buy everything I have, at a good profit, only I can get more by hanging on—why, what's the matter?"

Justine drew away from him, dabbed at her eyes, and then faced him squarely.

"Abel Smith! You're money-mad, that's the trouble with you!" she shot out. "You're just like those men rushing for the Sacramento! All you wanted was a farm—and now you have that, and you must have a lot more. All right, you can have it, but you needn't think you can have everything. You can have just five minutes to think it over."

"Think what over?" he asked in astonishment.

"Me. Either we get married and go to live on the farm, and do it now—or else we don't. Either you sell out your store, stocks and everything but your town lots, or else you can stay—by yourself." She looked up at the clock on the wall. "The five minutes has started, and at the end of it either I come first or not at all. So there."

Abel Smith swallowed hard and his Adam's apple bobbed.

She meant her words, and he knew it. Now he had the same choice as when he talked with Galbraith and Bennett. Quick wealth or certain and slow wealth—which?

The clock ticked off his thoughts, and he thought fast. Justine and the farm—or fabulous profits to be made here in San Francisco as the gold madness took hold of the world. Which? He had already turned a pretty penny. He could sell our to Sam Brannan and have enough to get going with the farm—

Money mad, was he? Maybe she was right at that. What good was gold to anyone? What good was wealth to anyone? Good in a way, perhaps yes; but the price might be too high. Frantic business deals, a life of rushing and fighting and conniving to make money—or peaceful quiet up along the brown hills, and all the dreams of farming come true, and a home where love was—

"Justine, I always did allow you had good sense," he said. She looked up at the clock, then turned to him.

"Well? Time's up, Abel."

He nodded. "All right. I've got one boat left. You say the word, and we'll pile our stuff into it tomorrow, get married and go up to the farm. Huh?"

Justine said the word—and Abel Smith never regretted it. Not even when, three years later, he sold his sixteen-dollar town lots for five thousand apiece, and put the money back into the finest farm in Sonoma County.

H. BEDFORD-JONES

B EDFORD-JONES IS a Canadian by birth, but not by profession, having removed to the United States at the age of one year. For over twenty years he has been more or less profitably engaged in writing and traveling. As he has seldom resided in one place longer than a year or so and is a person of retiring habits, he is somewhat a man of mystery; more than once he has suffered from unscrupulous gentlemen who impersonated him—one of whom murdered a wife and was subsequently shot by the police, luckily after losing his alias.

The real Bedford-Jones is an elderly man, whose gray hair and precise attire give him rather the appearance of a retired foreign diplomat. His hobby is stamp collecting, and his collection of Japan is said to be one of the finest in existence. At present writing he is en route to Morocco, and when this appears in print he will probably be somewhere on the Mojave Desert in company with Erle Stanley Gardner.

Questioned as to the main facts in his life, he declared there was only one main fact, but it was not for publication; that his life had been uneventful except for numerous financial losses, and that his only adventures lay in evading adventurers. In his younger years he was something of an athlete, but the encroachments of age preclude any active pursuits except that of motoring. He is usually to be found poring over his stamps, working at his typewriter, or laboring in his California rose garden, which is one of the sights of Cathedral Cañon, near Palm Springs.

Bedford-Jones has written stories laid in many corners of the earth, but among his most popular tales were the John Solomon stories which started many years ago in the *Argosy*.